I0650309

Maria Stella Ungern-Sternberg, Harriet M. Capes

The Memoirs of Maria Stella

Maria Stella Ungern-Sternberg, Harriet M. Capes

The Memoirs of Maria Stella

ISBN/EAN: 9783337540647

Printed in Europe, USA, Canada, Australia, Japan

Cover: Foto ©Andreas Hilbeck / pixelio.de

More available books at **www.hansebooks.com**

THE MEMOIRS OF MARIA STELLA
(LADY NEWBOROUGH)

Maria Stella, Lady Newborough, as a Gypsy.

From a picture at Glynllifon

THE MEMOIRS OF MARIA STELLA

(LADY NEWBOROUGH)

BY

HERSELF

*Translated from the original French by M. Harriet M. Capes
and with an introduction by B. D'Agen*

LONDON
EVELEIGH NASH
1914

LIST OF ILLUSTRATIONS

* The thanks of the publisher are due to the Hon. F. G. Wynn for permission to reproduce these pictures, and to Sir Ralph Payne-Gallwey, Bart. (author of *The Mystery of Maria Stella, Lady Newborough*: Edward Arnold), for the use of his copyright photographs of the same.

THE ORLEANS-CHIAPPINI CASE
NEWBOROUGH *v.* JOINVILLE

Whereas the plaintiff has claimed that the rectification of her certificate of baptism should be properly carried out, etc. That Lorenzo Chiappini, being near his death, wrote a letter to the plaintiff, in which, to ease his conscience, he declared that she was not his daughter.

That the words of a dying man must bear the impress of truth.

That, according to the evidence of the witnesses Bandini, it is absolutely proved that Count Louis Joinville exchanged his daughter for a boy of Lorenzo Chiappini's, and that the Demoiselle de Joinville was baptized under the name of Maria Stella, falsely described as the daughter of Chiappini and his wife.

That the Lady Maria Stella therefore justly claims the rectification of her birth-certificate.

Moreover, that the evidence of the aforesaid witnesses is supported by public notoriety and the difficulties the Comte de Joinville experienced.

Finally, that the legitimacy of the claim is proved by the careful education given to the plaintiff—an education unsuitable to the daughter of a jailer, as well as by the improvement in the fortunes of Chiappini which ensued.

For these reasons, which will be established both in fact and law by the proofs put in, and for all others resulting from the proceedings, it is held that the plaintiff's request should be granted, etc.

THE ORLEANS-CHIAPPINI CASE
JOINVILLE *v.* NEWBOROUGH

Whereas the plaintiff, in both her birth and baptismal certificates, is described as the daughter of Lorenzo Chiappini, who brought her up as such, and that so she acknowledged herself for nearly fifty years, etc.

That this plainly establishes the fact of her birth and consequent rights, etc.

That the proofs brought forward by the plaintiff amount to no more than the depositions of a few witnesses, whereas the proof should be in writing, etc.

That failing the necessary proofs of affiliation and paternity, the law holds good that given in the birth-certificate, etc.

That, even if the proofs given in evidence were alone sufficient, the witnesses produced by the plaintiff do not plainly report the fact of the substitution, etc.

Moreover, doubt is not dispelled by Chiappini's declaration, because it is not expressed in authentic or documentary terms, etc.

Finally, that to claim to be the daughter of a certain person not that named in the certificate of birth or shown as in possession, it is necessary to prove that such person has really existed, etc.

For these reasons, it must be held that the claims of the plaintiff be refused, and that she be condemned in all the costs of the trial, etc.

THE MEMOIRS OF MARIA STELLA

INTRODUCTION

In *Le Matin* of March 17, 1913, appeared the following article, with which we will begin the account of some abridged documents.

"While examining the Archives of the Office of Foreign Affairs, a young historian, M. Maugras, has unearthed a very curious love-story, deposited by the 'guilty couple's' own hands, relating to the Duke of Orleans, later Philippe-Egalité, and the governess of his children, the virtuous and pedagogic Mme. de Genlis.[1]

"In consequence of this *liaison*, Mme. de Genlis was made Captain of the Guards; and the 'governess' of the future Louis-Philippe and Mme. Adélaïde gave birth to two charming little daughters, who were brought up in England and known as Pamela and Miss Campton.

"Mme. de Genlis was also the mother of a legitimate daughter, who later on married M. de Valence. Mme. de Valence was to have for her son-in-law the Maréchal Gérard, lineal ancestor of the brilliant poetess, Rosemonde Gérard.

"On the other hand, Miss Campton married a Gascon, M. Collard, and was grandmother to Marie Cappelle (Mme. Lafarge).

"Thus, by legitimate descent, Mme. de Genlis is the ancestress of Rosemonde Rostand, and, illegitimate, of Mme. Lafarge.

"The latter wrote six thousand letters, not to speak

of her *Mémoires* and her *Heures de Prison*.

"As for the author of the play, *Un Bon Petit Diable,* 'he' proposed nothing less than to tune his pipe to all history and legend, in spite of what his own descent might imply....

"The heritage of the Governess of the Children of France has not fallen to the distaff side."

The next day, March 18, the same journal published this other article, which impartiality obliges us to reproduce here —

"Through the assiduous researches of a pious inquirer into the things of the past, the *Mercure de France* has just published a touching series of letters, written by Mme. Lafarge from her prison at Montpellier, to her Director, l'Abbé Brunet, residing in the Bishop's Palace at Limoges. This is a twofold revelation, in that it testifies both to the delicate skill of the writer and the innocence of the accused, but the correspondence is unfortunately incomplete.

"Some of these letters were given to M. Boyer d'Agen by M. Albris Body, Keeper of the Records at Spa in Belgium; others were discovered amongst the posthumous papers of Zaleski, the classic poet of the Ukraine; those that remain are doubtless buried in the dusty catacombs of some library.... It could be wished that one of those lucky chances which are the providence of the erudite might allow of their disinterment."

To complete this and prove something definite, these two quotations ought to be accompanied by a third which I take from one of the letters given by *Le Matin*, in which the celebrated Mme. Lafarge ventures to disclose the secret reason for her notorious misfortunes by at last revealing the mystery of her illegitimate origin, which, through the house of Orleans, of which her grandmother was issue, made her a near relation of Louis-Philippe, who during his reign, moved by fear, permitted the trial of this cousin by blood, whom he dared not have acquitted after ten years of imprisonment.

"The Queen charged the Maréchale Gérard," writes Marie Cappelle in this painful confession, "to tell me that she would make it her business to interest herself in me. She went herself to speak to the Ministers. It was last spring (1848), and the men condemned for the riots at Basanceney had just been executed. The Ministers said that there would be an outcry, that it would get mixed up with politics; *that the left-handed relationship* that was suspected would be exploited by parties and newspapers. In the month of August there was some hope; but the Praslin affair put a stop to everything. Now, I don't know what has become of the goodwill of our saintly Queen; I don't know if the Maréchale (Gérard) seriously means to carry out all the provisions of her poor mother's (Mme. de Valence) bequest. I have not written to her. It is painful to me to address prayers to men; I scorn to ask for pardon when I have the right to ask for justice."

The rest is known. Four years later, on June 1, 1852, Napoleon III opened a door Louis-Philippe had kept closed during the whole of his reign, and Marie Cappelle left her prison at Montpellier to go and die of exhaustion, four months later, at the little hot-spring town of Ussat, which could not give her back her lost life.

For my part, I was counting, letter by letter, the steps to Calvary climbed by this poor woman, and which, letter by letter, may be followed in a forthcoming book which is to contain all that I have been able to collect to the honour of this possessor of so fine an intelligence and so polished a style; when, all of a sudden, the episode of Marie Cappelle reminded me of that of Lorenzo Chiappini—with the house of Orleans as the origin of those doubtful births and as the clue to these yet unsolved historical enigmas.

What was the Orleans Chiappini affair?

In the spring of 1902 I was rummaging amongst the Archives of the Vatican, of whose secular secrets Pope Leo XIII, of august memory, had made an end by opening them to the world of inquirers, with no fear that the dangerous resurrection of this Lazarus of history would be for that liberal Pontiff—as it was for the Divine Miracle-worker of Bethany—the prelude to the maledictions of a scandalized Sanhedrin, and to another painful Passion—a renewal of that of old.

While waiting for the *crucifigation* of the Pharisees—those lovers of darkness and the unfathomable crimes of secret history—I took pleasure, as a simple Publican and lover of the light, in admiring the daylight making its cheerful way under the corniced vaults of the *Archivio Segreto*, and disclosing those files of dusty manuscripts, which, each stripping off his registered shirt, emerge naked from the tomb at the call of the first passer-by who, recognizing his dead, simply says, "Come forth!" and they come.

Standing before those desks over those deep tomblike cases of archives wherein slumber the secrets of the dead, my ears open to the miraculous, "Lazarus, come forth!" which the patient seekers for silent memories are prepared to utter at the turning of each yellow leaf, I let my dreaming eye, that afternoon, rest upon a ray of that Roman sunshine, as, with its soft radiance, it gave life to the solitude of a vault, scattering its riches broadcast through the windows, prodigal as the gambler staking with both hands just for the pleasure of playing, and losing.

"I've been using in your service the time you waste here!" said a searcher in this Vatican vault, as he came and sat down at my work-table. He is one who knows all the treasures of the place, since he has frequented it for over thirty years, working for the most learned of the best Reviews—the *Civilta Cattolica*, to which my honourable colleague is one of the most authoritative contributors.... "Well, what do they say in Paris about Louis-Philippe?"

"That he has been dead for some time!" I could not help answering, with a laugh at this not over-retrospective interruption.

"But is it known how he was born?" continued my interlocutor, more mysteriously than if he were simply talking nonsense; and without another word, "Here!" he added; "read this letter. I found it amongst the papers of Cardinal Joseph Albani, whom the celebrated Secretary of State Chateaubriand used to visit during his Embassy to Rome, and of whom he has left, in his *Mémoires d'outre-Tombe*, a witty enough portrait. Read this document; it is well worth while." In the Secret Archives of the Vatican it is inscribed (B. 43242, anno 1830)—

Cardinal Macchi to Cardinal Albani, Secretary of State.

"*Ravenna, Nov. 19, 1830.*

"Em^ss◎^me Maître,

"Enclosed in this letter you will find a copy of the

16

decision, given on May 29, 1824, by the Episcopal Tribunal of Faenza, in favour of the Lady Maria Newborough, Baronne de Sternberg, by the terms of which it is declared that this person is the daughter of the Comte and the Comtesse de Joinville, and not the daughter of the two Chiappinis. The documents concerning this affair are pretty numerous, but there is no mention made of the Orleans family. It is true that the aforesaid title of Joinville belongs to that Royal Family, and is borne at the present time, if I am not mistaken, by the daughter, born fourth of the family. It is true, likewise, that it is generally believed here that the Comte de Joinville was no other than the famous Duc d'Orléans-Egalité.

"Moreover, not only is there no proof that the Duc d'Orléans was travelling in Italy in 1773, but, on the contrary, we read in his biography that in 1778 he travelled in Italy in the company of the Duchess.

"I notice, besides, that Lady Newborough was born at Modigliana on April 17, 1773, and that the present King of France was born six months later. How, then, could the supposed exchange have been managed? It seems to me that this is a mere fable which might, and not a little, compromise us. I should advise your Eminence to claim those documents from the Tribunal of Faenza, so as to keep them from the public eye and in Rome.

"Having thus carried out your esteemed orders, I pray your Eminence to accept the humble expression of the profound respect with which, etc.

"Signed: V. CARDINAL MACCHI."

"But," said I, as I returned the folio to its obliging

discoverer, "it seems to me that this letter is conclusive, and that the Louis-Philippe Chiappini case is settled as soon as heard."

"Precisely, because it has not yet been heard. You are stopping your ears, like the *Eminentissimo* Macchi, Cardinal-Legate of Ravenna, who did not want to hear any more of the affair. But no, no!—and besides, you haven't the same excuse. Would you like, in connection with this letter, to read the document that goes with it? It is the Italian text of the sentence solemnly pronounced by the Episcopal Tribunal of Faenza, on the 29th of May, 1824; fifty years after this criminal business; all surviving witnesses heard; all inquiries scrupulously made; the Holy Trinity invoked in the name of the Father, the Son, and the Holy Ghost...."

"The devil!" I ventured to exclaim, at a matter beginning with so sacramental a formula.

And I read in Italian what I am going to give here in a translation, and the number of which, 43-242, is that of its place in the Secret Archives of the Vatican.

"Having invoked the most holy Name of God:

"We, seated in our Tribunal, and having before our eyes nothing but God and justice, by our final decision from the pleadings of the lawyers and the documents, we deliver judgment on the action or actions debated before us in the inferior or any other higher Court, between her Excellency Marie Newborough-Sternberg, the Plaintiff, on the one part, and M. le Comte Charles Bandini on the other, acting as legally delegated trustee to represent M.M. le Comte Louis and la Comtesse de Joinville, and any other absent person who has, or claims to have, any interest in the case; these two parties to it having submitted to jurisdiction, in default of the *Excellentissime* M. le Docteur Thomas Chiappini, domiciled at Florence, who has not so submitted himself.

"Whereas, before our Episcopal Curia acting as a Tribunal competent to judge the ecclesiastic cases named below submitted to their jurisdiction, the Plaintiff has asked that orders may be given, by means of suitable alteration, to correct her baptismal certificate, etc.

"That, on the part of the delegated Trustee Defendant, it is asked that the Plaintiff's claim should be rejected and the costs repaid. That the other proper Defendant, Doctor Chiappini, has not submitted to jurisdiction, though, according to the custom of this Curia, he has been twice summoned by a Sheriff of the Episcopal Tribunal of Florence, and that the report of contumacy has been added to the decision on the suit.

"Considering the documents, etc.

"Having heard the respective counsel, etc.

"Whereas Lorenzo Chiappini, being near his end, did, in a letter which was given to the Plaintiff after the decease of the aforesaid Chiappini, reveal to the same Plaintiff the secret of her birth, by clearly making known to her that she was not his daughter, but the daughter of a person he declared he could not name.

"That it has been legally acknowledged by the experts that this letter is written in the hand of Lorenzo Chiappini.

"That the word of a dying man is proof in full, since he has no longer any interest in lying, and it is to be presumed that he is thinking only of his eternal salvation.

"That such a confession ought to be looked upon as a solemn oath, and as a bequest made for the good of his soul and his own salvation.

"That the Trustee would vainly endeavour to deprive the said letter of its force, on account of its containing no indication as to who were the real father and mother of the Plaintiff; since although, in fact, such indication is really wanting, recourse has been had, on the part of this same Plaintiff, to the testimony of witnesses, to presumptions and conjectures.

"That, where there exists in writing a beginning of proof, as in the present case, it is allowable, even in State questions, to introduce testimonial proof and all other evidence.

"That if, in questions of State, after the original written proof, that by means of witnesses is admissible; there is still stronger reason to accept the same proof in this case when a document is produced to be used in the question of State.

"Whereas, from the sworn legal depositions of the sisters, Maria and Dominica Bandini, it is clearly shown that there was an agreement between M. le Comte and le Sieur Chiappini to exchange their respective children, should Mme. la Comtesse give birth to a girl and Chiappini's wife to a boy; that the agreed exchange did really take place, the case having been provided for; that the girl was baptized in the church of the Priory at Modigliana, by the name of Maria Stella, and falsely registered as the daughter of the Chiappini couple.

20

"Whereas the said witnesses swear as to the time of the exchange as coinciding with that of the Plaintiff's birth.

"Whereas, the Trustee, likewise in vain, urges the improbability of this evidence; since, not only no improbability is to be met with in the witnesses' statement, but, on the contrary, it is upheld and verified by a great number of other presumptions and conjectures.

"That one very forcible conjecture is deduced by the public voice and the rumours which were then spread as to the fact of the exchange.

"Whereas, this rumour is proved, not only by the testimony of the aforesaid sisters Bandini, but also by the attestation of M. Dominique Della Valle, and that of other witnesses in Brisighella and Ravenna, all equally judicially examined in their own towns and before their respective tribunals.

"That the vicissitudes to which M. le Comte was exposed are a convincing proof of the reality of the exchange.

"That there is documentary proof that in consequence of the rumours spread abroad in Modigliana concerning the exchange in question, the Comte de Joinville was forced to leave that place and take refuge in the Convent of St. Bernard at Brisighella; that having gone out for a walk, he was arrested, taken to, and kept some time in, the Public Palace of Justice of Brisighella, and that afterwards he was conducted by the Swiss Guards of Ravenna before his Eminence the Cardinal-Legate, who set him at liberty, etc., etc.

"Whereas, Querzani, of Brisighella, swears to

having shaved a great French nobleman who was for some time living in seclusion in the Convent of St. Bernard at Brisighella.

"Whereas, in the evidence of the aforesaid Della Valle, he declares that, while he was assisting in making out the inventory of the aforesaid Convent of St. Bernard, he saw two letters signed 'le Comte de Joinville'; that one of these was dated from Modigliana, and that in it the writer thanked the Abbot of St. Bernard's for having allowed him to retire into his convent; that, in the other letter, dated from Ravenna, the same correspondent tells of his liberation to the same Abbot; that both these letters bore the date of 1773.

"Whereas, one of the soldiers charged with the surveillance of the Count at Brisighella during his stay at the Palace of Justice of that town, is still living, which soldier has given evidence on the subject judicially and of his own free will.

"That M. le Comte Nicolas Biancoli-Borghi testifies in his judicial examination that, while he was looking through old papers of the Borghi house, he came upon a letter written from Turin to M. le Comte Pompeo-Borghi, the date of which he could not remember, signed Louis C. Joinville, which said that the *exchanged child was dead and that there was now nothing more to fear on its account.*

"Whereas, the same Count Biancoli-Borghi alleges his own knowledge to be the motive of his evidence, etc.

"That the exchange is proved also by the change in the fortunes of Chiappini, etc.

"That in fact, after this event, Chiappini paid ready

money for the cereals needed for the support of his family, and that he bought them at the Borghi place of business, while before that time he had discharged his debts by the giving up of his monthly pay; which Biancoli-Borghi testifies to having found as a fact in the books of the Borghi firm.

"Whereas, it is proved beyond doubt by many documents that Chiappini, after he retired to Florence, acquired means that enabled him to live at ease, as the sisters Bandini and other witnesses testify.

"Whereas, the Sieur Della Valle asserts that he saw Chiappini at Florence in flourishing circumstances, and that, moreover, the same Chiappini spoke of the exchange to a certain Sieur D. Bandini of Verifolo who was often in his company, as the same Bandini declared to Della Valle.

"Whereas, the Plaintiff received an education suited to her distinguished rank, and not such as would have been given to the daughter of a jailer, etc., etc.

"That, it clearly follows in view of all the matters up to now alleged and of many others existing in the documents, that Maria Stella was falsely described in her certificate of birth as being the daughter of the Chiappini husband and wife, and that she owes her birth to M. le Comte and Mme. la Comtesse de Joinville.

"That, in consequence, it is a matter of justice to grant the correction of the certificate of birth now claimed by this same Maria Stella.

"Finally, that M. le Docteur Chiappini, instead of opposing the claim, is guilty of contumacy.

"Having repeated the most holy Name of God, we

declare, decree, and give final judgment, that the pleas of the aforesaid delegated Trustee must be rejected, as we reject them; we desire and order that they be held as annulled; and, in consequence, we have declared, decreed and given final judgment, that the certificate of birth of April 17, 1773, inscribed in the Baptismal Registers of the Prioral Church of St. Stephen, Pope and Martyr, at Modigliana, in the Diocese of Faenza, wherein Maria Stella is described as the daughter of Lorenzo Chiappini and Vincenzia Viligenti, be corrected; and that, on the contrary, she is to be described as the daughter of M. le Comte Louis and Mme. la Comtesse N. de Joinville, French; to which end we have likewise decreed that the rectification in question shall be executed officially by our Registrar, also empowering M. le Prieur, of the Church of St. Stephen, Pope and Martyr, at Modigliana, in the Diocese of Faenza, to give copies of the rectified and corrected paper to all such as may ask for it, etc.

"LE CHANOINE PRÉVOT,

"VALERIO BOSCHI, PRO-VICAIRE GÉNÉRAL."

"The devil! the devil!" I repeated, astonishment increasing by leaps and bounds in the face of two such grave and contradictory statements. Was the Cardinal of Ravenna wrong? Was the Bishop of Faenza right? And did one ever see a scarlet-clad Eminence break a more vigorous rod over the violet-clad shoulders of a Counsel of Prelates than this reversion of a decree so solemnly pronounced, a few years earlier, before a plenary court of all the officers of a diocese?

"You forget," answered my colleague, "that the then Legate of Ravenna had been Nuncio at Paris under Charles X, and a special friend of the King's. So great a friend that the pasquinades on the Conclaves of 1829 and 1830, at which this Cardinal was present, always called him the *'Joueur de Gherardo della Notte,'* in memory of the royal card-parties at the château, where this ex-Nuncio was always the favoured partner. He was so loaded with presents, that the distended skirts of the prelate's gown became legendary in Paris as in Rome. And the least he could do amidst the amplitude of the cloth out of which he had shaped such a gown, was for the Cardinal Macchi to attempt later to shield the honour of the new King that, in this same 1830, Charles X, on abdicating, had left to France. But however deep they be, the well-furnished pockets of a modern Cardinal can't take the place of the ancient *oubliettes* of history."

"True! true!"

"To throw light upon this strange business, there is more than the affirmations of the Ecclesiastical Tribunal of Faenza and the denials of the Cardinal-Legate of Ravenna. There is a heap of proofs got together by the plaintiff in a voluminous memoir. Lady Newborough, Baronne de Sternberg, wanted it to be published in Italian and French at the same time. But the date of 1830, chosen for these startling revelations, was also that when the person principally interested mounted the throne of France. Is it to be wondered at that these compromising documents were at once destroyed wherever the representatives of the King Louis-Philippe could find them?"

"And then?"

"Then, there existed, and exists, a copy, thank God! Written in an elegant and easy hand, it once more proves the distinction of its author, as well as the sincerity of her words. You will easily discover the Italian text at Recanati, in the celebrated house of the Leopardis; for the Count Monaldo, father of the great poet Giacomo Leopardi, was not afraid of preparing an edition of this document for the edification of his contemporaries speaking the same tongue. The French text, which the supposed daughter of Philippe-Egalité undertook to publish in your language, and which she signed with the actual name of Joinville, which had at the first concealed the criminal *incognito*, would perhaps be more difficult to recover in France after the hunt for it But here is a copy which will console you for the loss of the rest. Shall we look through it together?"

"Certainly; it is enough that the Vatican should shelter such noble victims within the silence of its protecting walls, without Herod having to impeach the Pope for his guilty connivance in a repetition of the Massacre of the Innocents."

So here we are in the presence of Lady Newborough's Memoirs, which relate that she was born on April 17, 1773, at Modigliana; her supposed father being Lorenzo Chiappini, *sbirro*, or factotum, to the Count Borghi. Her supposed mother was one Vincenzia Viligenti, attached, as *concierge*, to the kind of prison of which her husband was warder.

This birth took place at the precise time that a certain Comte de Joinville and the Comtesse, his wife, who were staying at the Palazzo Borghi, opposite the prison of which Chiappini was warder, had also a child born to them. The child of Chiappini was baptized on the very day of its birth under the names of Maria Petronilla; *that of the Comte de Joinville does not appear in the Baptismal Registers of the Parish of San Stefano*, common to both families.

Maria Petronilla, always ignorant of her true origin and problematic destiny, lived until she was four years old between the indifference of her mother, who gave all her love to her other children, and the marked affection of the Countess Borghi, who greatly appreciated the natural distinction of the little girl, quite incompatible with so low an origin.

But the lowly estate of the Chiappinis improving day by day, Maria was only four years old when she had to leave for Florence, the Grand Duke having summoned the humble warder of the Modigliana prison to unhoped-for good fortune there.

Maria Stella's education kept pace with the growing prosperity of her father Lorenzo.

When the little girl had learnt enough of dancing and accomplishments, her father got her an engagement as ballet-dancer in a large theatre in the town.

Scarcely of marriageable age, she had first to spurn and then to accept the passionate addresses of an elderly English nobleman, who asked her hand. The parents granted what the daughter refused, and one day, against her will, Maria Petronilla became the wife of Lord Newborough.

Lady Newborough's Memoirs continue as tales of travel up to the page wherein she records the death of Lorenzo Chiappini, with this autograph letter from the dying man.

"MILADY,

"I have come to the end of my days without having ever revealed to any one a secret which directly concerns you and me.

"This is the secret.

"The day you were born of a person I must not name, and who has already passed into the next world, a boy was also born to me. I was requested to make an exchange, and, in view of my circumstances at that time, I consented after reiterated and advantageous proposals; and it was then that I adopted you as my daughter, as in the same way my son was adopted by the other party.

"I see that Heaven has made up for my fault, since you have been placed in a better position than your father's, although he was of almost similar rank; and it is this that enables me to end my life in something of peace.

"Keep this in your possession, so that I may not be held totally guilty. Yes, while begging your forgiveness for my sin, I ask you, if you please, to keep it hidden, so that the world may not be set talking over a matter that cannot be remedied.

"Even this letter will not be sent to you till after my death.

"LORENZO CHIAPPINI."

"Stranger and still stranger!"

"This letter, sent through the post from Florence to Lady Newborough, then at Siena, about the middle of December 1821, was the beginning of the lengthy investigations to which this daughter of noble but unknown parents henceforth entirely devoted herself. You must read the rest of the Memoirs, of which I venture to recommend whole pages to your consideration. Here is an extract—

"'After leaving my two eldest sons,' writes Lady Newborough, 'I took the road to Rome, where I had already made the acquaintance of Cardinal Consalvi, who showed me the greatest kindness. By his order, all the archives were thrown open to me; everything was examined into, not only in the capital, but in the country round about the Apennines; but everywhere the answer was the same: "Nothing whatever has been discovered; everything must have been destroyed during the Revolution."

"'Seeing that there was nothing to be done there, I set out for Faenza, where I was informed that the Count Borghi was absent, and that, moreover, it would be useless for me to see him, as he had declared that he would never tell me anything at all. I heard even that he had threatened the old servant-women with the withholding of their modest pensions if they had the ill-luck of speaking to me. But they could not restrain their longing to see me or the cry of their consciences. Their first words when they met me were a simultaneous exclamation of "O Dio! how like you are to the Comtesse de Joinville!"

"'I joyfully welcomed them and treated them kindly; and having implored them to acquaint me with the details concerning my birth, they at last consented to speak perfectly openly.

"'"Our father, Nicholas Bandini," they told me, "at the age of seventeen entered the Borghi mansion as chief steward, and never left it till his death. We also were taken on there in our youth as maids to the Countess Camilla. That lady, with her son, the Count Pompeo, was in the habit of spending a good part of the year at the castle at Modigliana, and in the beginning of the spring of 1773 we accompanied them there.

"'"On our arrival we found, already established in the Pretorial Palace, a French couple, called the Comte Louis and the Comtesse Joinville. The Comte had a fine figure, a rather brown complexion, and a red and pimpled nose. As to the Comtesse, you can see almost her perfect image in your own person, milady.

"'"Being such near neighbours, the greatest

intimacy soon came to pass between them and our masters. Every day the two families met, sometimes at one house, sometimes at the other.

""""The foreign stranger was extremely familiar with people of the lowest rank, especially with Chiappini, the jailer, who lived under the same roof. As it happened, both their wives were then *enceinte*, and the two confinements appeared to be imminent.

""""But the Comte was seriously anxious; his wife had not yet given him a male child; and he was intensely uneasy lest he should never have one, when of this very fear was born an idea, both barbarous and advantageous. First he broached the subject to the Count Pompeo and his mother, from a very charming point of view; then he endeavoured to worm himself more and more into the warder's confidence, and ended by telling him that seeing himself about to lose a great inheritance absolutely dependent on the birth of a son, he was quite willing, in case he should have a daughter, to exchange her for a boy, whose father he would largely recompense.

""""The man who listened to his words, delighted to find unlooked-for luck at so appropriate a moment, did not hesitate for an instant; he accepted the offer, and the matter was settled on the spot.

""""We know it," the sisters Bandini went on, "because we heard it with our own ears; and we know, too, that the event justified the precautions taken; the Comtesse gave birth to a daughter, and the other woman to a son. The news was brought to our master, and one of us going into the Pretorial Palace to see the newly-born children, was assured by some women of the house that the exchange had really taken place. Chiappini, who was present, confirmed it in his own words. Later on, the Countess Camilla often repeated it to us; she used to say that the Comtesse Joinville had been told all about it, and had seemed quite content.

""""Soon after this abominable crime we ourselves saw the Comte and the jailer on the best of terms; the first because he had secured immense profit; the other because he had received much money. Although silence had been promised, there were indiscreet people, and public rumour soon accused the authors of this horrible transaction. The Comte Louis, dreading the general indignation of his accusers, fled and hid himself at Brisighella, in the convent of St. Bernard. We knew he had been arrested and then set at liberty, but we never saw him again.

""""The lady left with her servants and her reputed son, while her own daughter, baptized by the name of Maria Stella Petronilla, and described as belonging to Lorenzo Chiappini and Vincenzia Viligenti, always remained with these last. Our mistress was constantly distressed about this misfortune. To repair it as much as possible she kept the unfortunate child near her, caressing her and giving her all kinds of presents, treating her not with ordinary friendliness, but with every mark of ardent love. So she behaved to this child for the first four years, that is to say till Chiappini took her with him to Florence, where he had her educated, and where he bought property with the price of his frightful bargain."

"'Thus spoke my venerable septuagenarians.

"'Fully satisfied with their story, there seemed no need of more, and that now it would be enough to appear before my iniquitous parents and obtain from them just reparation.

"'With this plan I set out for France with my third son, his drawing-master, my maid, and my courier, a faithful and intelligent servant.

"'By the Sieur Fabroni's advice, we went straight to Champagne, and the mere name of the place led us to Joinville. I asked the magistrates for information, and was told by them all that no nobleman of the neighbourhood bore the name of their city, and that it belonged solely to the Orleans family.

"'After several attempts, which all had the same result, I went to Paris, arriving on July 5, 1823. As a cleverly used ruse may bring about an act of justice, and as the bait of riches is nowadays the most powerful of motives, I had the following advertisement inserted in several newspapers—

"'"The widow of the late Count Pompeo Borghi has asked Lady N. S. to find for her in France a certain Louis, Comte Joinville, who, with the Comtesse, his wife, was at Modigliana, a little town in the Apennines, where the Comtesse gave birth to a son on the 16th of April, 1773. If these two persons are still living, or the child born at Modigliana, Lady N. S. has the honour to announce to them that she has been empowered to make them a communication of the highest interest. Supposing that these persons can prove their identity, they have only to apply to the Baronne de Sternberg, Hôtel de Belle-Vue, Rue de Rivoli."

"'Two days later appeared a colonel bearing the

much-desired name; I received him with the warmest welcome. He spoke, recounting his various titles. Alas! the one that had at first interested me so immensely was quite recent, and came to him from Louis XVIII.

"'At that moment I was told that M. l'Abbé de Saint-Fare solicited the honour of an interview; the colonel looked much astonished, and withdrew. In his place entered an enormous man, wearing spectacles and supported by two footmen. As soon as he was seated, the following conversation took place.

"'"The Duke of Orleans, having seen your advertisement, has this morning begged me to come and make inquiries about this inheritance; for we presume that that is the matter in question, and at the date you mention there was no one in existence outside the family to whom the title of Comte Joinville could belong."

"'"Was Monseigneur the Duke of Orleans born at Modigliana on the 16th of April, 1773?"

"'"He was born that year, but in Paris, on the 6th of October."

"'"Then I am very sorry that you should have taken the trouble to come; for in that case he has no connection with the person I am looking for."

"'"No doubt you have heard it said that the late Duke was very gay with the fair sex, and the child in question might well be that of one of his favourites."

"'"No, no, its legitimacy is incontestable."

"'"Could anything be more surprising! It is true, the late Duke lived in the midst of mysteries."

"'"Could you not describe him to me, Monsieur?"

"""Willingly, madame. He was a fine man with a good leg; his complexion was of a rather dark red, and, if it had not been for the numerous pimples on his face, he would have been very good-looking."

"""And his character?"

"""What people principally admired in him was his extreme affability to every one."

"""Your description agrees exactly with that that was given me of the Comte de Joinville."

"""Then it must be supposed that it was the Duke himself."

"""That can't be if it is true that his son was born in Paris."

"""May I ask you if there is a large sum to be had, and when?"

"""I am truly sorry not to be able to inform you; I am not at liberty to say more."

"'During the whole of this conversation, the big abbé had never left off looking at me in an almost offensive way; and, trying to find out what was my native tongue, he had spoken now in English, now in Italian, without being able to make up his mind, in consequence of my speaking both languages equally well.

"'After an hour's talk, he took leave, asking my permission to come again. I replied that I should be delighted to see him again, and, in my turn, begged him to be so good as to make inquiries amongst his many acquaintances.

"'He kindly promised to do so, and added that he knew a very aged lady from Champagne very well,

34

and that she might be able to give him much information, which he would transmit to me at once.

"'As nothing came of it, I sent M. Coiron, a teacher of French, who was giving lessons in it to my son, to him.

"'M. de Saint-Fare treated him politely, pleaded indisposition, and made great protestations.

"'On Coiron presenting himself a second time, he was received very coldly, and simply told that nothing had been yet done.

"'Moved by his own zeal and without my authority, he made a third attempt. Then the abbé told him plainly that he might discontinue his visits; that the lady knew nothing at all, and that he himself did not want to have anything to do with this fuss.

"'Still, the first impression his visit made on me could not be effaced. I procured a ticket, and went with my friends to the Palais Royal. What was my surprise on seeing in some of the portraits their extreme resemblance either to me or to my children. My astonishment increased when my young Edward, catching sight of a picture I had not yet noticed, exclaimed: "Dieu! Maman, how much that face is like old Chiappini's and his son's!"

"'We discovered that it was actually the portrait of the present Duke....

"'Thinking seriously over this, I realized that I owed to him in fact the important service of being the first to tear the impenetrable veil by deputing that Abbé de Saint-Fare, who, I was told, was not only his great friend, but his natural uncle, to see me.

"'It will be believed that, from that moment, all my

researches went in the direction so clearly pointed out....'

"The proofs Lady Newborough goes on heaping up in her startling Memoirs ought to be quoted as a whole," ended my guide, as he tied up the heap of papers. "But that will need another sitting, longer than the first. Here is the sun beginning to set, and the custodian of the Archives of the Vatican inviting us to go. Will this historical puzzle awake your curiosity? In that case you will have to endeavour to reconcile these undeniable yet contradictory documents, since they repose in the shadow of these protecting walls, where you may read on the face of the *Archivio* which Leo XIII set open for the truth of History, the proud device that bold and beneficent Pontiff had cut upon it when he invited the whole civilized world to enter its doors.

"'The first law of History is not to dare to lie; the second, not to fear to tell the truth; further, the historian must not lay himself open to a suspicion of either flattery or animosity.'

"The survivors of this domestic drama still draw breath at Modigliana and Brisighella, where Lorenzo Chiappini and Philippe-Egalité have left traces of their sojourn and their crime. At Glynllifon, in the Principality of Wales, the lineage of Lady Newborough, in the shape of her grandsons, still flourishes, if not the claims that died with her. Shall you go there, too, to examine into them?"

"Most assuredly," I answered; "for the honour of the blood of France, which cannot lie, and of the truth which could not well serve a nobler cause than this."

But, while waiting for the information which cannot fail to bring order and light into this still confused and perplexing affair, it was important that the actual text of

36

these Memoirs, hunted for by those interested in them for nearly two-thirds of a century, so that there is scarcely a copy left that is not worth its weight in gold, should be put in reach of honest minds which have likewise a full right to form an opinion on a case of such barbarity and of such national interest.

But what was to be expected of a Philippe-Egalité, who, to secure the great inheritance of Penthièvre, and needing a male firstborn, did not hesitate to sacrifice his own legitimate daughter for it? Would he be likely, a few years later, to hesitate before voting for the death of Louis XVI, who could no longer do anything for him? Had he not shown the extent of his complaisance in his preference for Madame de Genlis over his wife, whose confidante the mistress became under the very roof of the infamous husband of one and lover of the other?

The Memoirs of de Genlis have been widely read; let the Memoirs of Maria Stella be read likewise. After that we can talk with better knowledge of the facts.

BOYER D'AGEN.

FIRST PART
FROM MY BIRTH TO THE DEATH OF HIM I CALLED MY FATHER

———————————————————

I

I was born in 1773, in the little town of Modigliana, situated on the heights of the Apennines, which could be reached only by very bad roads. It belongs to the Grand Duchy of Tuscany, though dependent on the Diocese of Faenza in the Papal States.

On April 17 of the same year I was baptized in the parish church, receiving the names of Maria Stella Petronilla. My father's name was Lorenzo Chiappini; my mother's, Vincenzia Viligenti.

The family of Borghi Biancoli of Faenza owned, in my birthplace, a magnificent palace almost opposite the Pretorial Palace, where my father lived in the position of jailer.

The Count Pompeo Borghi, with his mother, the Countess Camilla, came there every year to spend the summer. The Countess happened to see me, and despite my father's ignoble profession, she was very fond of me and showed me immense kindness. I was admitted to her table, and often even shared her bed; she heaped presents upon me, and I lived almost entirely with her; I may even say that she inspired all the people of her house with the same sentiments, and that I was generally loved.

It was a precious compensation for the ills I suffered at home, where I had to endure the cruel brutality of a barbarous mother, to whom I was an object of detestation!

I well remember that as the first germ of gratitude developed in my little heart, I loved my benefactress as myself. When she was absent, I longed for her return, and when I had got her back, I couldn't tear myself away from her; in a word, she was all the happiness of my life; but, alas! it was soon to be torn from me.

I had not yet reached my fourth year, when my father was summoned to Florence by the Grand Duke Leopold, who put him in command of a company of archers (*capo squadra sbirri*). A few months later my father, in his turn, sent for us. I was his eldest child; two brothers were born after me, and the first had been dead some time.

The day we left, I was awakened very early, and in a few minutes my brother and I were each put into a pannier on a mule, and my mother got upon another animal of the same kind, our sole guide, protector and companion being the muleteer.

What tears I shed at leaving my dear Countess! It almost seemed as if I had foreseen that in losing this loving friend I should lose everything, absolutely everything!...

During the journey, which lasted two days, my mother seemed to care for nothing but my little brother, to whom she gave all her attention. Her neglect of me filled me with such bitterness that I felt like complaining to my father the instant we reached Florence.

In this new abode small-pox attacked our family; I got off with some small suffering; but my brother fell a victim to it, and my mother was not consoled for his loss till she gave birth to a third son six months later.

Scarcely convalescent, I was sent to a school, taken every morning by an ancient maidservant.

My appearance and manners, my native tongue, which nobody spoke at Florence; my rich attire, my splendid bracelets, my coral necklace, and all the gifts of the Countess Borghi, soon attracted much attention. I was sent for;

people were pleased to see me, and liked to listen to me.

But what struck other people so pleasingly made only an unfavourable impression on my mother; for the slightest fault I was punished with the greatest severity.

On one occasion she gave me such a violent blow with her heavy hand that I fainted, and, falling backwards, hurt myself terribly. When I recovered from my fainting fit, I could not restrain my grief. Going into a corner, I gave myself up to the most frightful despair, invoking my protectress with loud cries and calling to her for help.

Vain lamentations! Henceforth given over to my ill fortune, I was never again to find maternal consolation.

My father had a sister who was very unfortunate in her marriage; she left her husband and came to live with us. She and my mother could never get on; they detested each other, and were perpetually quarrelling.

Witnessing their disputes, my father sometimes took the part of one, sometimes of the other; still more often he reproved both of them, and drew their anger upon himself. The arrival of my paternal grandmother, who, growing old, came to be with her son, led to fresh subjects for wrangling; and as they were all violent and passionate, our house was like a veritable hell upon earth.

These interminable quarrels were not caused, as might be supposed, by the cares attending poverty. Though my father's post brought him in no more than a hundred francs a month, he had always plenty of money. He was well dressed, and often gave large dinners. He had abundance of provisions, and his cellar contained wines of the best kinds. He had a very pretty house and a splendid garden.

But these advantages were far from making up to me for my annoyances, or from doing away with the mortal weariness I felt in the bosom of my family.

I bewailed my fate unceasingly; I felt humiliated by my circumstances; I envied the ladies who possessed many servants, beautiful mansions, fine equipages, and most of all those who were received at Court.

These lofty aspirations were always with me; they were so deeply graven on my mind, so natural to me after a fashion, that I should have liked always to live with the great, and felt myself grievously hurt when I was obliged to keep company with common people.

I had, too, a decided taste for the fine arts; I had a passion for antiquities, and I do not doubt that I should have made great progress if my talents had been cultivated.

However, from the age of seven I was given lessons in writing, dancing, music, etc.

As my voice and my skill were remarkable, my parents made me early an object of speculation, and I was forced into practising cruelly. They made me sing, or play the piano eight hours a day, which inspired me with an insurmountable detestation of that instrument.

If my master complained of my inattention, I was shut up in the music-room from six in the morning till eight in the evening and given hardly anything to eat. If by chance I got a good report, I was pretty well treated, my father made me a present of twopence, and my mother told me ghost stories, which terrified me to such an extent that I scarcely dared to be alone during the night.

One day when they had forgotten to open my prison at the usual hour, I was suddenly seized with a panic of terror, and, quite beside myself, I opened the window and threw myself out into the garden, without doing myself any harm, however.

About this time great rejoicings were taking place in Pisa in honour of their Neapolitan Majesties, who were on a visit to the Grand Duke Leopold.

My mother, wishing to take the opportunity of going to see her sister, who lived in that town, my father gave his consent, on condition that my aunt and I should be of the party.

With what transports of joy did I receive this agreeable news! What a delightful and lively satisfaction it would be to let my *dear* piano rest!

Great preparations were made for my toilette; several frocks were bought for me; my father gave me two gold watches and a very valuable ring. He did not forget to make me take my shoes with their very high red heels, whose sound much delighted me.

We embarked on a public boat, and, although it was my first journey by water, my young imagination, far from dreading the perils of the furious element, was at once wonderfully diverted.

In twenty-four hours we landed at Pisa, where my uncle and aunt Fillipini, as well as their son and daughters, received us with open arms. They were greatly surprised to see me so richly clad, and said to my mother that no doubt her husband was very well off.

She answered only that I was a *bastard*, a name she gave me pretty often, and the meaning of which I did not understand.

Profiting by my father's absence to treat me with greater harshness, she was eternally scolding and tormenting me; she went so far as to take away my watches and my ring, to give them, as she said, to the great Madonna. Unluckily for me, she managed to procure a piano, at which I was pitilessly forced to work.

One day, having suddenly sent for me, she ordered me to sing for the amusement of two ragged and unpleasant-looking women she told me were intimate friends of hers.

Indignant at such a proposal, I said that a bit of bread was all they needed just at present.

She rose; I rushed to my room; but nothing could save me from her fury.

In vain did I beg her pardon, in vain entreated for mercy; a hail of blows fell upon me; my body was a mass of bruises; the blood streamed from my nose. I could not stand the overcoming pain; I went to bed, and did not rise from it again till we set out for Florence.

In this fashion my visit to Pisa became a real martyrdom for me instead of an amusement.

During my infancy I had been very subject to eruptions which from time to time appeared all over my body; but none had ever equalled that which was caused after my return by weariness and wretchedness. After the doctors had prescribed a lengthy course of cooling remedies, my parents, to rid themselves of such a nuisance, determined to send me to a hospital maintained at the expense of the Grand Duchess, and the admission to which needed great interest. Nevertheless, my father got an order without any difficulty.

I stayed there several weeks, and I must proclaim aloud that I felt as if I had refound my dear Countess in the person of each of the sisters who managed the hospital. Their constant care soon cured me; they were always near me, caressing me, and giving me fruit and sweetmeats.

No, no one could have been kinder, more courteous than those charitable women, to whom I vowed eternal gratitude, and whom I could not leave without anguish.

―――――――――――――――――――――

II

Nature had given me a good figure; nevertheless, my
father maintained that I stooped, that one of my shoulders
was higher than the other, and that my feet grew large too
quickly.

To remedy these imaginary defects he made me wear an
iron collar, which was taken off only at meal-time, a steel
corset that increased the torture and really made me
deformed, and shoes so narrow and short that I could
hardly walk.

When I begged him to take off this painful apparatus, a
box on the ear was his usual answer.

He often took me to the opera, to teach me, he said, to
hold myself properly; to move my arms easily; to behave
with grace.

All this rigmarole was an enigma to me, until at last he
explained it to me in these terms—

"Isn't it about time, my dear Maria, that you repaid what
I have spent on your education?"

"How can I do that?" I answered quickly, and with a
smile, "since all I have comes from you."

Instantly he replied—

"This is the way you are going to do it. I have got you an
engagement at the Piazza-Vecchia, where you will certainly

make a great success."

Dismayed by these words, I blushed, I trembled, and, concealing some of my trouble, I exclaimed—

"But the thing would be impossible. Don't you know, father, that the presence of two or three lookers-on is enough to confuse me when I am taking my lessons?"

Vain subterfuge.

"Make a beginning," he said harshly; "after you've done it a few times you'll find all the courage you need."

There was one last expedient left me. I flew to my mother and, with tears, begged her to remember how often she had told me that actresses deserved the most profound contempt. You may judge of my astonishment when I heard her answer thus—

"It was so formerly, my daughter; nowadays all that is changed; on the contrary, those ladies are admired and loved by everybody, and if they sing well they gain great wealth, and even sometimes marry great noblemen."

After that I saw there was nothing more to hope for; my doom was fixed and my misfortune inevitable.

I was made to study my part, which my unwillingness made a very slow business, and when the day for acting it arrived, my parents themselves came to introduce me.

When my turn came I found it impossible to open my mouth. My youth and my simplicity stirred the pity of the whole audience, while my father endeavoured to express his displeasure and anger to me by frightful grimaces, which at last forced me to stammer out a few notes.

The spectators made the building echo with their loud cries of *brava! brava! coraggio!* and at the end of the play several ladies of quality asked to see me, praising me repeatedly and lavishing all sorts of endearments upon me.

All the time the carnival lasted I was compelled to carry out the painful task imposed on me. One day, having tried to play the invalid, my father discovered the trick, and made me pay for it so dear that I did not again think of making that sort of excuse.

God alone knows how delighted I was when my engagement came to an end; but, alas! the relief was a short one. After a few months' rest, my father announced to me that I was about to have the honour of appearing on a larger stage, adding that everything was arranged and settled and there was nothing left for me but to obey his orders.

The news came upon me like a clap of thunder. Putting aside my nervousness, I felt myself degraded and debased.

More especially did I feel ashamed when I heard the actresses saying to one another: "It is disparaging to us to have the daughter of a constable put amongst us."

At this period I had two brothers and one sister, three little tyrants all of whose whims I had to humour; for if I made the smallest objection my mother encouraged them to abuse me and beat me, and throw stones at me. Fed and brought up delicately, nothing was good enough for them; but I had no difficulty, nevertheless, in realizing that they were being prepared for no better fate than mine, and they, too, were destined for my degrading profession.

Too unfortunate already in that I belonged to such a family, I was far from expecting fresh troubles, when my father read aloud to us the following letter, which he had just received, addressed to me—

"I have seen you, you beautiful star, and listened to the melodious tones of your angelic voice; they have intoxicated my heart. I implore you, my angel, to come at ten o'clock to the least frequented walls of the town; there you will receive the faithful promises of your unknown adorer."

This letter sent us into fits of laughter; my father alone was angry, and declared that if he could discover the impertinent author of such an anonymous letter he would severely punish him for his temerity.

The next day a messenger asked for me at the door. My father went in my stead, had a long talk with him, and I heard nothing further about it, till one day, having dressed me up like a goddess and given me all my mother's rings—carefully reduced in size with wax—to wear, I was told of the coming visit of an illustrious personage whom I was ordered to welcome.

At his arrival my parents bent themselves nearly double to show their respect, and motioned me to do the same.

I was inclined to mockery and could hardly contain myself, when I saw enter an old greybeard, from behind whose few and discoloured teeth came forth an offensive breath.

He was dressed in a blue coat braided with red, and wore a little white cloak with gold fringe, over which hung a thin queue, an ell long.

This gentleman, who, moreover, was stout, and might have been a fine-enough-looking man in his earlier years, introduced himself as Lord Newborough, an English nobleman, and, as he entered, told me he had come solely for the pleasure of hearing me sing.

How great was my reluctance to do as he asked! With what bad grace I sang!

My *bravura* ended, I made some excuse and retired.

A few days later milord appeared again; his visits became

more and more frequent; soon they were daily.

Each time he talked to me of his wealth; boasted of his immense possessions; gave me the most magnificent descriptions of England; and was constantly repeating that he was a widower with only one son.

His Italian was so bad that I should never have understood his jargon without my father's help.

I understood no better why I was always so well got-up, so adorned with jewels and diamonds. When I asked the reason, I was told that all this finery would induce the great lord to increase the value of the presents he could not fail to make me.

In vain I did my utmost to convince my parents that I hated the very idea of receiving the least thing from him. They overwhelmed me with reproaches, asking me if this was the way I meant to repay them; representing to me that they had to provide for the education of three other children; and at last saying plainly—

"How would it be if you had to marry this man whom you had no right to look for, and who is so much above you?"

Unhesitatingly I cried, "O Dio! Dio! I would rather die!"

Then my father bade me remember that his power over me was absolute and that I was bound to obey his commands; my mother joined in and declared, with an oath, that, willing or not, I should be the wife *del signore inglese*.

Realizing that it was not a joke, I implored them to let me become a nun, or to do with me what they pleased so long as I was not forced to make such a detestable match; but my words, my tears, my sighs, resulted only in making them more angry and eliciting more hateful oaths.

Then I ran to my grandmother and my aunt, begging

them to take my part. They did as I asked, but without success; they were only forbidden to mention the subject again.

Wounded to the very depths of my heart, I gave myself up wholly to my grief, scarcely alive or able to breathe.

Milord himself came to rouse me from my stupor.

At the sight of him I gave a wild cry, and, falling at his knees, with sobs implored him not to exact such a sacrifice from me; to think of my youth; to see that I could not reasonably give my hand to a man old enough to be my grandfather and for whom I felt an insurmountable aversion.

He did nothing but laugh at my pitiful simplicity; and, raising me from my lowly attitude, he said to me that if I did not love him yet, I would later on; that his rank, his estates, his wealth, and all the fine things I should enjoy, would oblige me to love him dearly.

At these words my whole being was possessed by fury; I violently thrust back my insupportable persecutor, looking at him with blazing eyes; I abused him, passionately declaring that I would rather endure any plague than the union he offered me; that I would rather face all the miseries in the world; that death itself would be nothing to dread; that, besides, my hatred of him had come to its height; that it was so deeply rooted in my heart that nothing could tear it up, and that my greatest happiness would be to be rid of his presence for ever.

III

Arrangements with Milord—His Son—Brain-fever—Fruitless

Though my engagement at the theatre was to end in a fortnight, my father got a substitute for me, and himself gave up his post; maintaining that all that was henceforth incompatible with the high rank I was to attain.

Nevertheless, he did not forget to take his precautions, but effected an agreement greatly to his own advantage, and, with no thought for my future, simply put me at the mercy of my elderly adorer in consideration for a sum of fifteen thousand *francesconi*, a pension of thirty ducats a month, and the proprietorship of a magnificent country house at Fiesole, very well furnished, with a courtyard, gardens, and two immense vineyards.

Moreover, milord promised to pay the expenses of the whole family during his whole stay in Italy on condition that he and his son were allowed to live with us.

That young man was then sixteen years old, tall and well made; Nature had endowed him with ability and a good heart, but he was so ignorant and uncouth that it was pitiful to see him. He could neither read nor write, and used the coarsest expressions; his greatest pleasure was the company of low people or servants.

He talked a great deal about a Signora Bussoti, wife of milord's cook, telling any one who choose to listen that this *very respectable* person had caused his mother's death, and was daily eating up his father's fortune; that she had children whose legitimacy was anything but certain, and for whose sake he himself had often been beaten.

These speeches, and many other blemishes I caught sight of through the trouble my future husband took to prevent my being entirely disgusted with him, finished by making me realize completely the depth of the abyss into which I was to be thrown. My youthful imagination took fright, and I could no longer bear the weight of my misery.

All at once I was seized with violent pain, my senses were benumbed, my head turned, and for twenty-six days my life was despaired of. Even in my delirium the thought of my unhappiness did not leave me; I cried aloud; I breathed complaints; I made incoherent murmurs. My grandmother and my aunt were inconsolable; they were always with me, and their constant and affectionate care greatly contributed to my recovery.

Alas! as soon as I recovered consciousness, I regretted that I was alive; I rose and rushed to the balcony; but my father came in, took hold of me and stopped me.

Vainly I took the opportunity to repeat my humble remonstrances and to swear perfect obedience to him in every other respect; he only put before me, in his turn, all the supposed advantages I should gain, and averred that the Grand Duke, knowing all about me, absolutely required me to be ennobled.

As soon as I was well enough to go out, the doctors advised country air, and we went to Fiesole, a little town three miles from Florence.

There a new idea came to me, which at first I believed might be very useful. I urged the difference of religion and the impossibility of my marrying a Protestant.

But the old heretic did away with that difficulty at once.

"I'll turn Jew!" he exclaimed; "I'll turn Mussulman; I'll turn idolater; I'll turn anything you like so long as you'll consent to be my wife."

And he called in priests and monks to instruct him, and neglected nothing necessary for becoming a member of the

Roman Church.

After that there was nothing to be done but fix the day for my immolation.

The fatal day arrived, and by the first light of dawn we made ready to start for Florence.

Before getting into the carriage, for the last time I threw myself at the feet of my inexorable parents, watering them with my tears, while sobs choked my voice.

My mother grew angry and heaped abuse on me; my father raised me roughly, saying crossly, "The Grand Duke wishes it; there's no way of going back now."

We set off at once, and fearing that the populace might rise against the unjust violence done to a girl of thirteen, we went not to a public church but to a private chapel.

I was led to the foot of the altar and placed by the side of the man I abhorred.

Questioned by the minister, I had nearly answered in the negative, when my father pinched me, and, with a muttered threat that he would kill me, somehow extorted from me the fatal vow which put the seal on my wretched fate.

The ceremony over, we returned to Fiesole, where a number of friends came to offer their congratulations.

Instead of receiving them, I shut myself up in my room, and it was in vain that they sent for me. I took no food but what my grandmother and aunt brought to me in secret.

At the end of four days my father burst open the door, forced me to go out, and put me into the arms of my husband, or rather my insufferable keeper; for he was so full of jealousy that he could not endure the presence of a man. If I went out, he wanted to accompany me, or sent some one after me.

Scores of times he was guilty of rudeness to people who honoured me with their salutations, and on every hand he thought he saw favoured rivals or dangerous emissaries.

Every day the fumes of wine upset his weak mind; he gave way to frightful fits of anger, and after having infinitely increased the usual discomforts of our dreary household, he would fall into a deep sleep in which he snored loudly.

He speedily conceived such an antipathy for the various members of my family that he never spoke of them but by the most filthy names.

When I reminded him of the affectionate and loving names he constantly called me by, he always answered, "As for you, my dear better-half, you may feel quite sure there is nothing in common between your charming self and that odious stock."

And truly I was often astonished myself that there was so obvious a difference, whether in the colour and shape of the face, whether in the disposition and temperament, the bearing and speech, or the mental faculties and the inclinations of the heart.

The contrast was especially striking between my generosity and the well-known avarice of the Chiappinis.

They were in constant torment from this passion; they were for ever exhorting me, urging me to ask for money, to demand ornaments, to go to shops to buy them whatever they wanted.

My humouring them, their own extravagances, and, even more, the insatiable claims of the *charming* Bussoti, soon exhausted the exchequer of milord, whose credulity let him be robbed of nearly his last farthing.

I don't know what would have become of him if Mr.

Price, his man of business, had not opportunely arrived.

This gentleman handed over some ready money to him, and prepared to return and send him back some larger sums.

There was waiting, and impatience, and counting of days and hours! At last the post brings a letter. My father goes to fetch it, breaks the seal, has it translated, and its contents are known before it reaches the person to whom it is addressed.

It announces the sending off of several trunks. Joyful news! Clapping of all hands!

But what a surprise! When the trunks, so longed for, were opened, nothing was to be seen but a heap of old rubbish that Mr. Price had doubtless got together from the wardrobes of milord's grandmamas, and by which he had thought he might temporarily assuage the raging thirst of my greedy relatives.

I could not help laughing, while my mother, bawling at the top of her voice, accused me of carelessness, declaring that if there was nothing better, it was because I had not been willing to ask for anything.

IV

Return to Florence—Rupture and Reconciliation—The British Minister —English Lady's-maid—Milord's Imprisonment—My Flight— Presents and Promises—My Father's Avowal—My Behaviour Towards Him—His Obliquity.

My husband soon wearied of the country and wanted to return to Florence. There he hired a fine house, big enough to hold us all; the first storey was to belong to him, his son and me; my parents occupied the second. We were to be independent of each other, but Lord Newborough was still responsible for the expenses of the double household.

Although forty-five years old, my mother was then *enceinte*, and gave birth to a fifth boy, who was named Thomas, after milord, his godfather.

LORD NEWBOROUGH

FROM A PICTURE AT GLYNLLIFON

The education of my brothers took a quite different direction from what had seemed probable at first. My husband placed them in a large school, with his own son, who could not stay there more than a few months.

Afterwards an attempt was made to give him a tutor; but the young man was irrevocably ruined. When the tutor saw him he said, "I have come too late."

In changing my abode I had in no way changed my situation; milord kept up his usual style of living, giving me endless trouble; and those who ought to have been a comfort to me, treated me with contempt, only saying, "Really, you are not worthy of your lot; don't you understand that you are on the eve of becoming a very wealthy widow, and that soon you will be able to do just what you please?"

But in spite of these fine words, they did not show themselves very willing at times to put up with the fits of rage of the irascible old man.

One day, when the intoxicating fumes had got greatly into his head, he provoked my father by his abuse and rushed at him to strike him. Armed with a big stick and wild with rage, my father vigorously returned the assault, till the noise they made and their outcries attracted a crowd which separated them.

The assailant left his house and ordered me to follow him. As I clearly and positively refused to do so, I received a note in which he informed me that if I did not do as he asked, he should put an end to his life. I seized a pen and wrote him these few words—

"My old fool, if you wish to give me a proof of your affection, make haste and carry out what you announce to your unhappy victim,

"Maria."

Several days went by without my hearing anything about him, and I was almost happy; but this calm was but the prelude to the storm.

One of his servants came to tell me that he was dangerously ill, and that, feeling his last hour to be at hand, he begged to see me that he might make important communications to me.

It was in vain I answered that I had no wish to receive any; my father pointed out to me that such conduct on my part could not fail to be very prejudicial to us.

He added that he would go with me, and swore that he would bring me back with him.

Reassured by this promise, I agreed, on condition that our visit should be a short one.

As I entered, I was greatly astonished at seeing the British Minister beside milord's bed.

The supposed sick man held out his hand to me and assured me that it needed only my presence for his complete recovery; that he was very sorry for having given me so much trouble, and that it should not happen again.

"I wish you good health," I replied quickly; "but to return to you is quite impossible; and I declare to you that if it had not been to please my father, you would never have seen me here."

I got up at once, and signed to my father to leave.

He did not stir; his look revealed the plot to me, and I realized his deceitfulness.

The Minister did all he could to lessen my vexation, and averred that he took upon himself the responsibility for the conduct of my husband in the future.

From that moment that gentleman showed me much attention; he introduced me to his wife, and procured me the acquaintance of several English ladies, among others the

Misses C., with whom I became very intimate, especially the second, afterwards the Marchioness of B., my greatest friend.

Still I had to endure numberless mortifications; the Italian nobility looked down on me, and milord was invited by himself to the great receptions. Moreover, my domestic circumstances had become more unbearable than ever.

My husband had insisted on giving me a lady's-maid of his own country and choice, the most worthless of women. In a short time she had succeeded in wholly captivating her old master, and even more, his son, so that she ruled despotically in the house; nothing was done without her, her advice was received like an oracle, and her words were commands no one dared disobey. If I allowed myself a comment, she treated me like a child, and took pleasure in secretly taunting me with my lowly origin and the contemptible part I had played in my own despite. I could not take a step without having her at my heels, finding fault with everything I did; and as my most innocent doings were always malignantly misconstrued, I made up my mind to give up all outside amusements.

Keeping to my own room, I had no recreation but music and the care of my birds.

One day when I was petting my favourite sparrow, they came to tell me that milord was asking for me to go out driving with him. I went down, quite resolved to make my rightful complaints to him....

Our carriage, having crossed the town, was stopped at the barrier. We went to another of the gates and were treated in the same fashion.

My husband, in a fury, accused Chiappini of this, and swore to have his revenge. He forbade me to hold any communication with him, and ordered his abominable confidante never to let me out of her sight. Paying no attention to his reproofs, I went back quietly to my room.

Suddenly there arose a great uproar in the next room; I opened the door and saw milord, followed by three constables, who seized him and dragged him away to the fortress.

The lady's-maid screamed aloud and hurled a torrent of abuse at me.

The next morning she received a letter and went to the prison, after putting me in charge of two footmen, who took advantage of her absence to empty a bottle or two.

Having myself taken the opportunity to go out on my balcony and breathe freely, a note which I saw came from my father was thrown up to me. Joyfully I picked it up.

It told me to hold myself in readiness at a certain hour.

I hastily put on all my most valuable things, and at the appointed moment went quickly downstairs and jumped into a carriage that was at the door. There I found my aunt, who tenderly welcomed me, and in no time we reached Fiesole, where my father told me that, having heard by public report that my husband wished to get away without paying his debts, he had got leave from the Grand Duke to have him put into safe keeping.

Walking in the garden on the Sunday, I saw the arrival of his son, who, as he met me, said,

"Milady, allow me to offer you some trifles my father sends you."

I declared that I would take nothing from him, and that his gifts were as hateful to me as their giver.

But the parcel had already fallen into the hands of my mother, who welcomed its bringer with jubilation, and begged him to repeat his visits.

"Oh, how beautiful!" she cried as she opened the box; "who would have believed milord had such good taste? I'll wager that several of these fine things were bought for me."

I retorted that she might take them all, and that never in my life would I touch one of them.

It needed nothing further to induce her to take possession of the whole lot, except the flowers, which she looked upon as worthless.

The same messenger reappeared towards the end of the week, and handed me the following letter —

"My angel, I cannot live without you. Oh! if you knew how I weary for you, I am convinced your tender heart would break. Come, come, to comfort me. Happiness awaits you with me. A large sum of money is being sent to me to meet all my obligations, and we will leave Florence soon and go to my own dear country, where you will be admired by all the world, especially by your humble and affectionate slave."

While reading these curious sweet things, I had noticed the delight of my family at hearing that a large sum was coming from England, and in it I saw the omen of a distressful reconciliation.

My father left us at once, and the very same evening I had the misery of seeing him return with milord, who fell at my feet, saying, "Dear jewel of my heart, behold your faithful adorer."

At the same time he offered me a bouquet, which I threw in his face.

Far from being offended, he pressed me to his bosom; and while I struggled to free myself, my father joined in, declaring that he had no power over my person, that he could not keep me away any longer, and that the law obliged me to live with my husband.

I felt my blood freeze in my veins; I gave full vent to my indignation; I stated its causes unreservedly; but the only satisfaction I could obtain was the dismissal of my infamous persecutrix.

***

V

Integrity of Milord—Preparations—Secret Union—Stay at the Hague —Arrival in England—The Country of Wales—My Exaltation— My Griefs—My Relations—The Eldest of my Brothers.

The pretended report of Lord Newborough's projected flight was a pure invention of my father's; for I feel bound to say to the credit of the first that his integrity stood all proof, and that his too great generosity placed him infinitely above any suspicion of meanness. If he had prolonged his stay in Italy, it was simply to enable him to meet all his family's engagements by cutting off for a time a host of superfluous expenses his presence in his own country would have necessitated.

Mr. Price had written that he was coming to us; he came, and the preparations for our journey were begun; the accounts were all made up, all engagements were met. My father received his 15,000 *francesconi* and all the arrears of his pension. It was settled that he should accompany us to Boulogne, and that my aunt should go with us to England.

As we were to travel by land as far as the Hague, my mother managed to instil into us a dread of robbers, and insisted on keeping back some of my diamonds to wait for a safe opportunity for sending them direct to me. I need not say that she never found it!...

On the eve of our departure it was perceived that the son of milord was missing; he was called for, sought for, in vain. My father set to work all the constables of his acquaintance, and one of them at last succeeded in discovering him with my former maid, who had fainted. He protested that he would never abandon his *lawful wife*; but as this wonderful title rested on nothing more than a kind of clandestine marriage, the Archbishop of Florence promptly absolved him from his vows. He was made to listen to reason, and some assistance was given to the forsaken beauty.

On leaving this town, I felt the liveliest regret at the separation from my grandmother, who had always been so kind to me; as for the rest of my family, indifference was all they aroused in me.

At Boulogne I took leave of my father, who, as a final consolation, assured me I should become a maid-of-honour at the English Court, and acquire all the titles that had belonged to Lady Catherine Perceval, Lord Newborough's first wife.

When we reached the Hague, Mr. Price left us to make preparations in London and Wales.

We took up our quarters in an hotel, and my husband hastened to leave his card on the British Minister, who, being absent, was represented by Lord H. Spencer, son of the Duke of M., who came to call on us, and offered to present me to the Dutch Royal Family, who received me with extraordinary affability.

He also made me acquainted with several of the best families, and my stay in Holland was a round of drives, games and amusements.

When we had been there six months, Mr. Price wrote that everything was ready for our reception.

When we arrived in London, my husband introduced me under the name of the *Marchesina di Modigliana*, the name I still bear in the English Court Circular.

As it was summer, and the greater number of the best families were in the country, there were but few ladies for me to meet, amongst whom I was especially attracted by Lady Ford, and we became very intimate friends.

After spending a couple of months in the capital of the British Empire, we set forth for Wales, where Lord Newborough's largest estates and his finest mansion, called Glynllifon, were situated. Glynllifon is about six miles from Carnarvon in North Wales, and in that town we had the most magnificent reception; the horses were taken out of the carriage, and the young men dragged us in their place. We were escorted home by six hundred men, all people or friends of milord's. In the evening our park, as well as the town and the surrounding estates, were brilliantly illuminated and filled with a vast crowd that begged at intervals to be allowed to look at me. When I complied with their wishes, the air was rent with loud applause.

All the noble families of the neighbourhood came to call on us, and for six consecutive months it was like a perpetual *fête*, and we had as many as fifty guests every day.

GLYNLLIFON

FROM A DRAWING BY THE LATE SIR JOHN ARDAGH

Towards the end of the winter we went back to London, where my act of naturalization was at once set about. As my husband had arranged everything beforehand, there was no difficulty about the matter, and in less than a month the necessary preliminaries for my presentation at Court were accomplished.

I was presented by Lady Harcourt, chief lady-in-waiting to the Queen, and was received with the most wonderful marks of regard and admiration. My dress of cloth-of-silver, adorned with precious stones, dazzled everybody, and I was regarded with the greatest interest.

From that moment I had the entry into the highest society, and, instead of the humiliations I had so often experienced at the hands of my compatriots, I found myself surrounded by respect and honour.

Personages of the highest rank sought my acquaintance, and thought themselves happy to be received by the wife of a noble peer, illustrious descendant of the ancient Princes of North Wales, and grandson of the intimate friend of George I.

In spite of all this, I was far from tasting the sweets of happiness; my aversion for the man to whom I owed all these good things made me envy the lot of women belonging to even the lowest classes of society.

My only consolation was in pouring out my griefs to my aunt, and even that comfort I was to lose. She had never been able to get used to either the climate or the customs of my new country; absolutely ignorant of its language, she could not join in any conversation, and, rosary in hand, from morning till night she told her beads.[2]

As her health visibly declined, I felt obliged to give way to the wish she had long expressed to return to her native land; but her departure filled me with sadness and trouble, and I could not endure the thought that the protectress of my childhood would no longer be with me.

I insured her enough to live upon in comfort, and handed over to her several trunks, either for herself or for my other relatives, from whom I was always receiving importunate requests, and to whom I constantly replied by the perpetual sending of packets.

More than half the pin-money milord allowed me went to Italy, not to speak of the goods of all kinds I was always sending to the same destination.

Not content with all this, my father sent us his eldest son, who was a pretty good historical painter, and begged us to look after him. We kept him with us for a year, and then my husband sent him to the East Indies, where he cost us a heap of money, as Messrs. Coutts & Co. of London can testify.

He stayed three years in Calcutta, and then went to the Cape of Good Hope, where he married the daughter of the Danish Consul, to whom Lord Newborough had given him an introduction. His wife's brother taking him into partnership, in a short time he made a large enough fortune to be able to enjoy all the comforts of life and to bring up his numerous family, consisting, I believe, of fourteen children.

VI

Consumption—Death of my Step-son—Birth of my Children—The
Arrival of Several Members of my Family—Domestic Cares—
Milord's Death—My Second Marriage—Much Travel—Fresh
Sojourns in Italy—My Third Brother—My Behaviour to my
Father—His Death.

The eruptions which had been so great an affliction in my
childhood continued making their appearance at intervals;
but when I was twenty-six, the evil having settled on my
chest, it was believed that I showed strong symptoms of
consumption. I was so weak that after walking a few steps I
could not breathe; bathed in a cold sweat, I could get no
rest.

Several remedies were tried on me without any good
result. The doctors advising change of air, we set out for
Wales; but it was soon seen that that cold and damp climate
was more hurtful than helpful to me. Not knowing what
else to do, I was ordered to Tunbridge Wells, and it was that
marvellous specific that gradually restored me.

I was still only just convalescent, when milord's son was
himself attacked with a decline, which carried him to his
grave.

His constitution had been a robust one, but long
undermined by his own errors it could not make any
resistance. He succumbed, after every medical expedient had
been tried in vain.

His father was broken-hearted; in addition to the loss of
his only son, he saw that his vast estates would pass to

relations of whom he had good reason to complain.

To provide against this misfortune as much as possible, he made a will to the effect that, if he should die without issue, the larger part of his property should go to the second son of the Minister, Perceval, brother of his first wife, leaving me at the same time an annuity of £1400, on condition that I granted him a favour, until then persistently refused....

His grief was so great, and he had always shown me so much kindness, that at last I felt it to be my duty to make the most painful sacrifices for his sake—I consented to become a mother!...

With what transports of gratitude did he not welcome the first signs of the fulfilment of his hopes! But even they did not equal his delight when I gave birth to a son. Beside himself with joy, he ordered that no expense was to be spared, and gave the most brilliant of entertainments; the best families came to it and offered us their heartiest congratulations.

As for myself, I felt then the most delightful emotion, quite new to my heart and which I recognized as maternal love.

This happiness was increased the next year by the birth of a second son, whose baptism was celebrated with great pomp. Mr. Perceval and Lord Bulkeley were his godfathers.

My father, having heard that I was now sole mistress in my husband's house, hastened to bring his daughter, to give me, as he said, a pleasant companion.

They both appeared in sailor costume, which made me feel greatly ashamed; and I had them dressed in a proper fashion.

My father ran all over London, visited all the places of interest, laid his hands on everything he could get in our house, and departed with well-lined trunks.

I kept my sister with me, furnished her with a magnificent wardrobe, and gave her in abundance everything she could desire; but in spite of it all, I could never conquer her hardness of heart, and every day she distressed me by her constant rudeness.

Her connection with Lord Newborough brought her in contact with a distinguished ecclesiastic, whom she subsequently married.

We had just heard that my second brother had got into terrible trouble in Italy, when he made his appearance in order to secure himself from the hands of justice, which would have infallibly consigned him to the same fate as one of his cousins, who was sent to the galleys for ten years.

My consternation may be imagined!

My husband was furious, and expressed very forcibly to me his disgust at being so tormented by this *insaziabile canaglia*, as he called it. I was almost as angry as he; nevertheless, I did my best to quiet him, thinking to do good to my brother; but his bad conduct soon obliged us to send him away.

I got him placed with a merchant at Leghorn, but he, too, could not keep him for more than a few months.

Since my father's visit I noticed that milord often forbad me to go to entertainments frequented by the French nobility, especially the Bourbon Princes.

This fresh antipathy greatly amused me, though I wondered over so odd a warning; since at that time I was living in absolute retirement with my children. Having no thought but for them, I lavished endearments on them and all the care their growing infirmities needed; for I had the grief of seeing that I had bequeathed them a very sad inheritance. The eruptions which had caused me so much suffering made their appearance very early on their little bodies; the eldest was quite covered with them. Many remedies were tried, but the root of the evil was never wholly destroyed.

Although their father had never suffered in a similar way, his health, shattered by other causes, gave way completely; he fell ill of a terrible disease which lasted a year and ended in his death. In the midst of his severe pains he would take no help but mine; he gave me constant marks of love, and to give it effectual expression he considerably increased my annuity.

It was in my arms that he drew his last breath, on the 11th of October, 1807.

His funeral was solemnized with all the pomp befitting his rank and fortune; all the people of distinction made a point of attending it and did not fail to pay their touching tributes of condolence to my grief.

The deceased had assigned for his children's education a sum which was thought insufficient; a larger was put at my disposal by the Lord Chancellor; but it was ruled that I should lose it, as well as my guardianship, if I married again.

My youth was so far past that at first this condition seemed useless and ridiculous to me.

Meanwhile, I went to drink the waters at Cheltenham, and there I met a Russian Baron, called Ungern Sternberg, who paid me immense attention; I was charmed with his kindness, enchanted with his fine manners. He loved music, dancing, riding, and a hundred other things I, too, liked. This peculiar similarity of tastes brought us together and soon formed a strong tie between us.

Later on I met him in the best houses in London, especially and on several occasions at that of General Hughes, whose wife constantly entertained me with accounts of the wonderful merits of the gentleman, never tiring of exalting his talents and virtues.

Thinking she saw that I thoroughly agreed with her, she told me that he intended to ask for my hand. Such an idea never having entered my head, I looked upon it as an idle tale and laughed at it. But she returned to the charge; her husband joined in, and the Baron himself made me a formal offer.

Seeing that this was a serious matter, I did not hesitate in giving an absolute refusal; alleging my position with regard to my two sons.

Every possible step was taken to make me believe that it would be easy for me to obtain permission to retain all my rights over them.

My objections were contested so cleverly; I was so lulled with hopes; such earnest and well-worded entreaties were made to me, that it became well-nigh impossible to make any further opposition. I yielded, and made up my mind to contract a second union which everything around me combined to represent to me in the most tempting light.

My consent given, my future husband went to carry the news to his own family, while I went to Lady Charlotte Bellasis, my late husband's niece by marriage, at Newborough Park.

The Baron joined me there, and our wedding was celebrated on the 11th of September, 1810.

Immediately afterwards we returned to London to prepare for our departure.

I will not attempt to describe the grief I felt at having to dismiss my servants; still less will I try to describe the anguish of my heart when I realized that it was vain to dream of keeping the guardianship of my children. Milord's executors were inexorable, they tore them from me.

Having left at the beginning of November, we travelled across Switzerland in severe cold, and did not arrive in Petersburg until the last fortnight of January.

Count Pahlen, our uncle, First Minister to the Emperor, received us in the most friendly fashion; he introduced me to the highest society, and, but for the bitter coldness of the weather, I should have taken part in all their gaieties.

If I was not presented at Court, it was because, as an English lady, such a presentation should have been made by the English Ambassador, and at that time there was not one, in consequence of the war between the two countries.

Nevertheless, I was admitted to look on at a brilliant entertainment inside the Palace; and the Emperor Alexander, having noticed me amongst the other lady spectators, commanded his first gentleman-in-waiting to show me all the splendours of that delightful residence.

Everything I looked at, and still more the universal courtesy of manner, promptly convinced me of the great mistake it is to look upon the Russian nation as behindhand in European civilization.

Spring having brought back warmth, we went to Reval, to offer our respects to my mother-in-law, who welcomed us warmly, and showed me much kindness.

A little later we set sail for the Island of Dago, where lay the Baron de Sternberg's principal estates.

All his acquaintances there received me with enthusiasm, and did their best to divert my mind; but with no success until the birth, in the following month, of a third son, whom I called Edward, after his father.

How can I describe what this newly-born son was to me, especially when his first signs of intelligence made me foresee that he would become more and more worthy of my love?

Feeling unable to let him be out of my sight for a moment, I took him with me the first time I went to see his brothers.

I had the comfort of finding them pretty well in health; but alas! it was but too evident to me that perfidious skill had been at work in filling their minds with unjust prejudices against her who had always loved them so tenderly. In spite of their goodness of heart, they could not help showing a certain coolness which greatly grieved me.

I set to work to revive their old love for me, and flatter myself I succeeded.

At the end of a year my husband came to fetch me in one of his own vessels, manned by his own people, in which I lived as in a house of my own.

While in England I had been given several very great curiosities, among others a fan from the East Indies and a magnificent bird-of-paradise feather; I added to these a little piece of work I had made out of the rarest shells then known, and took the liberty of sending the whole to her Majesty the Empress Elizabeth, who most graciously had a delightful and flattering letter written to me, and sent with it a magnificent clasp set with brilliants.

But I will tell nothing more of my return to Russia nor of another journey to England I made. Let us go back to my parents.

My father had written to me of the deaths, one after another, of my second brother, my grandmother and my mother; and he was constantly expressing the most intense wish to embrace me once more before he himself followed them to the grave.

At last I yielded to his pressing entreaties, moved greatly by a vague hope I had always kept of seeing again the old Countess Borghi, of whose death I had never positively heard.

When I got to Italy I made inquiries about her which resulted in my hearing that she had died when I was scarcely nine years old.

My father, aunt and brother joined me at the hotel where I had put up for the time; they were all in excellent health.

My brother became my intimate confidant; I told him all my affairs and put all my concerns into his hands, delegating my authority to him.

Very soon I noticed that he was received very coldly in the good houses to which I took him; I asked one of my old friends the reason for this, to be told by her that the young man, having behaved very badly during the course of his studies at the University of Pisa, where he took his degree in Law, had brought back with him a doubtful reputation, which day by day grew worse.

My own experience promptly showed me that these suspicions were far from being without foundation; and thenceforth I left off confiding in him....

For two consecutive years I took every care of my father; not only did I provide for his wants, but I invited him to my table; I desired him to come to the parties I gave; I tried to cheer him up by my talk; I made much of him; while, on his side, he always showed me the most profound respect, never calling me anything but milady, and behaving to me like a humble retainer.

In vain I implored him to remember that I owed my existence to him; to call me his daughter and to treat me like one; I saw that my loving reproaches awoke no sweet transports of paternal affection. He scarcely ventured to look me in the face, and spoke only of his gratitude, constantly repeating that I had been his lucky star and mumbling the word "Borghi" and another that he never finished.

This confusion and these many mysterious speeches seemed to me the signs of approaching mental aberration and made me very uneasy.

At last he fell dangerously ill, and I was inconsolable. I sent for doctors; I got three attendants for him, and ordered that he was to have every comfort.

MARIA STELLA, LADY NEWBOROUGH

FROM A BUST AT GLYNLLIFON

One day they came to tell me that on recovering from a
sudden attack he had uttered my name and asked to see me.

I flew to his bedside, kissing him and weeping over him. He looked at me with eyes full of sorrow, pressed my hand, and struggled hard to make himself understood; but his paralysed tongue refused to articulate anything but: "*Mio Dio!*—Barant, Baranto——"

I was overcome with grief at his state; I was advised to go; they led me away and put me into my carriage.

On the morrow my brother sent me word that the poor dying man being no better than on the previous day, a visit from me could not fail to be hurtful rather than helpful. On the following days he wrote to me in the same fashion, and at last came himself to tell me, with every sign of grief and affliction, that our father was no more.

SECOND PART
FROM THE DEATH OF HIM I HAD BELIEVED MY FATHER UNTIL THE PRESENT TIME

I

My brother appeared to be so much affected by his recent loss that, in spite of the coolness existing between us for some time past, I kept him to sleep at my country house.

All the evening he seemed to be sunk in deep thought and overwhelming grief, which greatly surprised me in a young man who up to then had shown so many signs of a want of filial affection. He left very early the next morning without taking leave of me.

I at once sent him the sum necessary for having the funeral solemnized in a fashion in accordance not with the lowly condition of the deceased, but with all the dignity due to my own rank.

The marble beneath which lie his mortal remains bears witness to my liberality, very unlike that of my sister, who, being present at her mother's death, allowed her body to be cast into the common pit, when a dozen crowns would have procured her a more honoured grave.

My constantly recurring eruptions had induced my

79

doctors to prescribe sea-bathing; my father's illness having deferred the carrying out of their orders, I prepared to do so a fortnight after his death, which took place towards the end of January 1821, and went to spend three weeks at Leghorn, where I should have been horribly bored if it had not been for the company of my Edward, who never left me.

On my return to Florence I found out the various tricks my brother had played on me, first in concealing from me the real condition of my father, who, I learnt, had recovered his power of speech before breathing his last, and whose death had not taken place until thirty-six hours after the time reported to me; secondly, in persuading me to pay the purchase money of a fine house, supposed to be for me, but the deed of purchase of which he had had made out in his own name, on the pretext that a married woman could not do so validly.

Justly incensed at his conduct, I not only upbraided him bitterly, but ignominiously cast him out and gave him up absolutely and finally.

Surrounded as I was by nothing but gloomy memories, in a place where everything recalled troubles and misfortunes, I resolved to go to Siena, and began at once to make my preparations.

There were several reasons that induced me to fix on that town, among others its pure air and the famous School of Design which is its chief ornament.

I was well acquainted with the head master of this school, and he had kindly promised me to take the greatest pains with my young son, who already showed decided taste and talent for this admirable art.

I had been living in this town about a week when I received by post the letter I give here, with its translation.

Miledi.

Giunsi finalmente al termine di miei giorni senza vere svelato ad alcuno un segreto che riguarda me e la vostra persona direttamente.

Il segreto è l'appresso:

Il giorno dell a vostra nascita da persona che non posso nominare, e che già è passata all' altra vita, a me pure nacque un figlio maschio. Fui richesto à fare uno scambio, e mediante l emie finanze, di quei tempi, accedi alle molteplici richieste con vantaggio; ed allora fù che vi adottai per mia figlia, in quella guisa che mio figlio fu adottato dall' altra parte.

Vedo che il cielo ha supplito alle mie mancanze, con porvi in uno stato di miglior condizione del vostro padre, sebbene esso pure fosse per rango quasi simile, ed è ciò che mi fa chiudere con qualche quiete il termine di mia vita.

Serva a voi questa operazionne per non farmi colpevole, totalmente; domandovi perdono di questa mia mancanza, vi prego, se vi piace, di tenere in voi questa cosa, per non far parlare il mondo di un affare che non vi ha più rimedio.

Non vi sara consegnata questa mia che dopo la mia morte.

Lorenzo Chiappini.

Milady

I have come to the end of my days without having ever revealed to any one a secret which directly concerns you and me.

This is the secret. The day you were born of a person I must not name, and who has already passed into the next world, a boy was also born to me. I was requested to make an exchange, and, in view of my circumstances at that time, I consented after reiterated and advantageous proposals; and it was then that I adopted you as my daughter, as in the same way my son was adopted by the other party.

I see that Heaven has made up for my fault, since you have been placed in a better position than your father's, although he was of almost similar rank; and it is this that enables me to end my life in something of peace.

Keep this in your possession, so that I may not be held totally guilty. Yes, while begging your forgiveness for my sin, I ask you, if you please, to keep it hidden, so that the world may not be set talking over a matter that cannot be remedied.

Even this letter will not be sent to you till after my death.

LORENZO CHIAPPINI.

The amazement such a missive caused me may well be imagined. In an instant a crowd of ideas rushed upon me; the veil was rent, the cloud dispersed. At once I realized the reason for the immense differences between myself and my supposed relatives.

I saw the reason for the ill-treatment I had endured at the hands of a woman perhaps forced into calling herself my mother; I understood the meaning of those many muttered enigmatical half-sentences of my first husband, and still more those of the writer of the astounding letter I held in my hand.

There was but one mystery left to clear up, and that was precisely the one I was implored to let alone.

But the man who had so implored me was now in my eyes nothing but a criminal for me to forgive, his paternity destroyed, his rights broken, and my duty to him annihilated, or rather born anew—enjoined on me by honour and the love I bore my children—namely, to try every possible means to discover my real father.

In my anxiety I hastened to the postmaster, as if he were the person to give me useful information; but all he could tell me was that the letter in question had come in the bag from Florence and under the postmark of that town; but he directed me to an old man, a native of Faenza, to whom I went at once. He could tell me nothing at the time; but he wrote, and received an answer that there were two maid-servants of the Countess Camilla still living, and that there was a new Count Biancoli-Borghi, a relation and heir of the Count Pompeo, whose widow he had even married.

For my part I had written to the Fathers Ringrezzi and Fabroni, the first-named confessor to the former jailer, the other the nephew of the confessor of the late old Countess.

Having accepted the invitation I sent them to come and see me, Father Ringrezzi told me at once that his calling bound him to inviolable secrecy, but added that his private opinion had always been that I was the child of the Grand Duke Leopold.

At this, Father Fabroni eagerly exclaimed—

"You are wrong, Monsieur l'Abbé. Milady is the daughter of a French nobleman, called the Comte Joinville, who had great possessions in Champagne; and I have no doubt that if Madame la Baronne went to that province she would find documents that I have been told were handed over to a worthy ecclesiastic."

On this combined advice, I decided to return at once to Florence to get further information. I had the satisfaction of finding no incredulity; my many friends all told me that they had never believed I belonged to the family of the Chiappinis.

I was told that the constable, having at one time been in danger on account of his political opinions, had entrusted the lady Massina Calamini with some papers which he told her were of the highest importance, and which he carefully reclaimed the very moment he was set free.

It is equally certain that he had a great number in a strong box, the key of which he never gave up to any one whatsoever.

But it was impossible to get anything from his son, except a few letters of no consequence, which he had already shown me with a laugh as being the only asset of his inheritance.

As to her whom up to now I had called my aunt, she came to see me several times, and I continued to look after her welfare.

It seemed to her that her brother had been quite capable of the thing he had so tardily confessed to me; she even maintained that she remembered his wife, in her fits of rage often throwing these cutting words at him—

"You monster! Have you forgotten that you've committed a crime worthy of the gallows?"

Count Borghi and the two old maid-servants living at Faenza having been applied to for information, the latter replied that first of all they wished to see me and to speak to me alone; the Count indignantly asserted that I had made an unpardonable mistake about him, and swore that he would make me pay dearly for it.

Not knowing what more to do, I went and asked a clever lawyer what steps I ought to take. He told me I must submit

Chiappini's letter to the authorities and have it legally verified.

As this verification entailed great formalities and much delay, I went back to Leghorn to continue my sea-bathing. I soon heard the news that my two elder sons were coming to visit me; my heart overflowed with joy; I hastened to meet them, and received them at Florence.

They rapturously embraced me and gave me a thousand proofs of their love for me. We spent five delightful weeks together, and about the middle of November they started for Rome. I could not accompany them; my presence had become indispensable to accelerate my business, which still lasted more than another month.

At last the experts, having carefully compared the writing submitted to them with several authentic signatures, decided that it was entirely in the hand of Lorenzo Chiappini.[3]

As soon as this was finished, I hastened to join my children, and managed to arrive on the first day of the year 1823, so as to give them my presents and renew the heartfelt proofs of my love for them, which they received with touching gratitude and profound respect.

The first thing they told me of was their fortunate meeting with my old and most faithful friend, the Marchioness of B., who was looking forward with the liveliest impatience for the moment of my arrival. My delight was at its height; seeing her once more seemed to give me back a part of myself.

They went very fast—those happy days I spent with her and my three children.

Obliged to return to England, she gave me two letters of introduction to use after the journey to France which I intended to make; one was for the Duke of Orleans, the other for the British Ambassador.

She earnestly begged them to give me their powerful assistance, and, moreover, entreated the first to be so kind as to present me to his sister, who, she said, would soon become my friend, since my features and manners were exactly like hers.

My son was close upon one-and-twenty, and was bound to be in London on the 3rd of April, the day he would attain his majority, in order to take his seat in Parliament.

Consequently, he and his brother left Rome about the end of February. I went with them to Florence, to Pisa, and to Leghorn, and there I said my last farewell to them.

Never was anything sadder or more harrowing than this cruel separation; a secret presentiment warned me, alas! that it would be but too long a one.

II

Return to Rome—Departure from Florence—Testimony of the Sisters Bandini—My Arrival in Champagne and in Paris—An Innocent Ruse—Colonel Joinville—The Abbé de Saint-Fare—Visit to the Palais-Royal—My Reflections—Lady Stuart—Advice.

After leaving my two eldest sons, I took the road to Rome, where I had already made the acquaintance of Cardinal Consalvi, who showed me the greatest kindness. By his order, all the archives were thrown open to me; everything was examined into, not only in the capital, but in the country round about the Apennines; but everywhere the answer was the same: "Nothing whatever has been discovered; everything must have been destroyed during the

Revolution."

Seeing that there was nothing to be done there, I set out for Faenza, where I was informed that the Count Borghi was absent, and that, moreover, it would be useless for me to see him, as he had declared that he would never tell me anything at all. I heard even that he had threatened the old servant-women with the withholding of their modest pensions if they had the ill-luck of speaking to me. But they could not restrain their longing to see me or the cry of their consciences. Their first words when they met me were a simultaneous exclamation of "O Dio! how like you are to the Comtesse de Joinville!"

I joyfully welcomed them and treated them gently; and having implored them to acquaint me with the details concerning my birth, they at last consented to speak perfectly openly.

"Our father, Nicholas Bandini," they told me, "at the age of seventeen entered the Borghi mansion as chief steward, and never left it till his death. We, also, were taken on there in our youth as maids to the Countess Camilla. That lady, with her son, the Comte Pompeo, was in the habit of spending a good part of the year at their castle of Modigliana, and in the beginning of the spring of 1773 we accompanied them there.

"On our arrival we found, already established in the Pretorial Palace, a French couple, called the Comte Louis and the Comtesse Joinville. The Comte had a fine figure, a rather brown complexion, and a red and pimpled nose. As to the Comtesse, you can see almost her perfect image in your own person, milady.

"Being such near neighbours, the greatest intimacy soon existed between them and our masters. Every day the two families met, sometimes at one house, sometimes at the other.

"The foreign stranger was extremely familiar with people of the lowest rank, especially with Chiappini, the jailer, who lived under the same roof. As it happened, both their wives were then *enceinte*, and the two confinements appeared to be imminent.

"But the Comte was seriously anxious; his wife had not yet given him a male child; and he was intensely uneasy lest he should never have one, when of this very fear was born an idea, both barbarous and advantageous. First he broached the subject to the Count Pompeo and his mother, from a very charming point of view; then he endeavoured to worm himself more and more into the warder's confidence, and ended by telling him that, seeing himself about to lose a great inheritance absolutely dependent on the birth of a son, he was quite willing, in case he should have a daughter, to exchange her for a boy, whose father he would largely recompense.

"The man who listened to his words, delighted to find unlooked-for luck at so appropriate a moment, did not hesitate for an instant; he accepted the offer, and the matter was settled on the spot.

"We know it," the sisters Bandini went on, "because we heard it with our own ears; and we know, too, that the event justified the precautions taken; the Comtesse gave birth to a daughter, and the other woman to a son. The news was brought to our masters, and one of us going into the Pretorial Palace to see the newly-born children, was assured by some women of the house that the exchange had really taken place. Chiappini, who was present, confirmed it in his own words. Later on, the Countess Camilla often repeated it to us; she used to say that the Comtesse Joinville had been told all about it, and had seemed quite content.

"Soon after this abominable crime we ourselves saw the Comte and the jailer on the best of terms; the first because he had secured immense profit; the other because he had received much money. Although silence had been promised, there were indiscreet people, and public rumour soon accused the authors of this horrible transaction. The Comte Louis, dreading the general indignation of his accusers, fled and hid himself at Brisighella, in the convent of St. Bernard. We knew that he had been arrested and then set at liberty, but we never saw him again.

"The lady left with her servants and her reputed son, while her own daughter, baptized by the name of Maria Stella Petronilla, and described as belonging to Lorenzo Chiappini and Vincenzia Viligenti, always remained with these last. Our mistress was constantly distressed about this misfortune. To repair it as much as possible she kept the unfortunate child near her, caressing her and giving her all kinds of presents, treating her not with ordinary friendliness, but with every mark of ardent love. So she behaved to this child for the first four years, that is to say, till Chiappini took her with him to Florence, where he had her educated, and where he bought property with the price of his frightful bargain."

Thus spoke my venerable septuagenarians.

Fully satisfied with their story, there seemed no need of more, and that now it would be enough to appear before my iniquitous parents and obtain from them just reparation.

With this plan I set out for France with my third son, his drawing-master, my maid, and my courier, a faithful and intelligent servant.

By the Sieur Fabroni's advice, we went straight to Champagne, and the mere name of the place led us to

Joinville. I asked the magistrates for information, and was told by them all that no nobleman of the neighbourhood bore the name of their city, and that it belonged solely to the Orleans family.

After several inquiries, which all had the same result, I went to Paris, arriving on July 5, 1823. As a cleverly used ruse may bring about an act of justice, and as the bait of riches is nowadays the most powerful of motives, I had the following advertisement inserted in several newspapers—

"The widow of the late Count Pompeo Borghi has asked Lady N. S. to find for her in France a certain Louis, Comte Joinville, who, with the Comtesse, his wife, was at Modigliana, a little town in the Apennines, where the Comtesse gave birth to a son on the 16th of April, 1773. If these two persons are still living, or the child born at Modigliana, Lady N. S. has the honour to announce to them that she has been empowered to make them a communication of the highest interest. Supposing that these persons can prove their identity, they have only to apply to the Baronne de Sternberg, Hôtel de Belle-Vue, Rue de Rivoli."

Two days later appeared a colonel bearing the much-desired name; I received him with the warmest welcome. He spoke, recounting his various titles. Alas! the one that had at first interested me so immensely was quite recent, and came to him from Louis XVIII.

At that moment I was told that M. l'Abbé de Saint-Fare solicited the honour of an interview; the colonel looked much astonished, and withdrew. In his place entered an enormous man, wearing spectacles and supported by two footmen. As soon as he was seated, the following

90

conversation took place—

"The Duke of Orleans, having seen your advertisement, has this morning begged me to come and make inquiries about this inheritance; for we presume that that is the matter in question, and at the date you mention there was no one in existence outside the family to whom the title of Comte Joinville could belong."

"Was Monseigneur the Duke of Orleans born at Modigliana on the 16th of April, 1773?"

"He was born that year, but in Paris, on the 6th of October."

"Then I am very sorry that you should have taken the trouble to come; for in that case he has no connection with the person I am looking for."

"No doubt you have heard it said that the late Duke was very gay with the fair sex, and the child in question might well be that of one of his favourites."

"No, no; its legitimacy is incontestable."

"Could anything be more surprising! It is true the late Duke lived in the midst of mysteries."

"Could you not describe him to me, Monsieur?"

"Willingly, madame. He was a fine man, with a good leg; his complexion was of a rather dark red, and, if it had not been for the numerous pimples on his face, he would have been very good-looking."

"And his character?"

"What people principally admired in him was his extreme affability to every one."

"Your description agrees exactly with that that was given me of the Comte de Joinville."

"Then it must be supposed that it was the Duke himself."

"That can't be if it is true that his son was born in Paris."

"May I ask you if there is a large sum to be had, and when?"

"I am truly sorry not to be able to inform you; I am not at liberty to say more."

During the whole of this conversation, the big abbé had never left off looking at me in an almost offensive way; and, trying to find out what was my native tongue, he had spoken now in English, now in Italian, without being able to make up his mind, in consequence of my speaking both languages equally well.

After an hour's talk he took leave, asking my permission to come again. I replied that I should be delighted to see him again, and, in my turn, begged him to be so good as to make inquiries amongst his many acquaintances.

He kindly promised to do so, and added that he knew a very aged lady from Champagne very well, and that she might be able to give him much information, which he would transmit to me at once.

As nothing came of it, I sent M. Coiron, a teacher of French, who was giving lessons to my son, to him.

M. de Saint-Fare treated him politely, pleaded indisposition, and made all manner of excuses.

On Coiron presenting himself a second time, he was received very coldly, and simply told that nothing had yet been done.

Moved by his own zeal and without my authority, he made a third attempt. Then the abbé told him plainly that he might discontinue his visits; that the lady knew nothing at all, and that he himself did not want to have anything to do with this fuss.

Still, the first impression his visit made on me could not be effaced. I procured a ticket, and went with my friends to the Palais Royal. What was my surprise on seeing in some of the portraits their extreme resemblance either to me or to my children. My astonishment increased when my young Edward, catching sight of a picture I had not yet noticed, exclaimed, "Dieu! Maman, how much that face is like old Chiappini's and his son's!"

We discovered that it was actually the portrait of the present Duke....

Thinking seriously over this, I realized that I owed to him in fact the important service of being the first to tear the impenetrable veil by deputing that Abbé de Saint-Fare, who, I was told, was not only his great friend, but his natural uncle, to see me.

It will be believed that from that moment all my researches went in the direction so obviously pointed out, and, above all, that I took good care to keep possession of the letter the Marchioness of B. had given me for *his Highness*.

As for that she had been good enough to write about me to the British Ambassador, I myself left it with my card at the door of his house. A week later, his wife, Lady Stuart, simply sent her name by a footman as sole answer; which greatly astonished me from a lady of title, a relation of my friend's and daughter of the Earl and Countess of Hardwicke, with whom I had been formerly very intimate.

I was advised that, finding no support in that quarter, and having henceforth to fight against wealth and power, I had better go back to Italy to take every necessary measure and to collect all quite authentic documents.

III

My Return to Faenza—First Visit of the Count Borghi—His Story—
Public Rumours—Evidence of Messieurs Valla, Guerzani,
Tondini, Ludovichetti, della Valle, Perelli and Maresta—My Letter
to the Count—His Second Visit—Legal Formalities—Judgment in
my Favour—Decree of Rectification.

Before leaving France, I made several discoveries which
more and more strongly confirmed my suspicions as to the
personality of the Comte Joinville. But my first object being
to find proof of the exchange itself, I went again to the place
where it had been effected.

As I passed through Turin, Alessandria, Reggio, etc., I
employed several people to make inquiries for me. At
Modena I made the acquaintance of the lawyer, Massa, who
had a great reputation, and who clearly marked out for me
the course I ought to take. At Bologna I engaged an
advocate whom this gentleman had recommended to me;
but I was soon obliged to give him up on account of his
dilatoriness, and replaced him by the Signore Bucci, of
Faenza.

When I arrived at that town, I went to stay with the
Marchesa di Spada, to whom I had an introduction.

As she was very intimate with Count Borghi, I had
conceived the hope of obtaining through her useful
information, and especially the return of certain papers that
gentleman, it was said, boasted of having in his possession.

She wrote to him, but there was no answer. I then called
upon the Bishop of the diocese, claiming from him a
perfectly impartial investigation of my case, assuring him
that I asked for nothing but justice, and entreating him to
persuade the Count to accept my invitation.

The prelate strongly backed my request, and Count
Borghi, not daring to refuse him, at last came to see me,

bringing with him an enormous packet of letters which he declared he had received from me. They bore the fictitious name of my so-called man-of-business, and were evidently written with the intention of incensing against me a man who might prove so helpful to me.[4]

My astonishment was beyond words, and I made such eager protestations of my innocence in the matter that he was quite convinced of the truth, and spoke to me as follows —

"I have often had occasion to look over old papers belonging to the Borghi family, of whom I became the representative; and one day when I was doing so at Modigliana I saw a letter addressed to the late Count Pompeo, dated from Turin and signed *Louis, Comte de Joinville*, the contents of which, so far as I can remember, were as follows —

"'Since we left that place, my wife, always prolific of girls, has at last presented me with a boy. As to the one of whom you know, there is left only the grief of having lost him, and I feel no *further scruples* on his account. My compliments to your ladies, and believe me, etc.'

"This letter greatly struck me, and I examined it more than once; but then I considered it of no importance, and I ended by tearing it up, without attempting to remember the date."

"In the account-books of an old steward, which I looked over likewise, the name of the jailer, Lorenzo Chiappini, was often written; and I noticed that before 1773 this person bought his necessary provisions of the Borghis, by relinquishing a part of his future salary; while, after that time, he always paid in ready money for corn and wine of the best quality. These account-books could not now be discovered, because when I had looked through them I gave them back to the aforesaid steward, who is no longer living."

Who could believe that, with no motive, this gentleman could have parted with papers relating to an inheritance just fallen to him, and which he had looked into minutely? Still less, who could believe that he could have destroyed a paper that had so greatly interested him, that he had read several times, and whose tenor was so deeply graven on his mind?

Nevertheless, in order to prove to me that he now bore me no ill-will, he bestirred himself to make others speak.

Very soon the voice of the public was quite on my side; every one knew of Chiappini's sudden accession of wealth; every one remembered hearing something about the Signore Joinville and his excessive familiarity.

It was generally assumed that the jailer's wife, going to her Easter confession a few days after the exchange, had been ordered by her director to denounce its principal perpetrator to the Holy Office. It was said that this Tribunal, having ordered his arrest, the Count had been warned, and fearing the probably unpleasant results of this order, had asked and obtained permission to take refuge in a convent at Brisighella until the storm had blown over.

It was affirmed also that, having ventured to go out for a walk, he was seized and taken to the Town Hall, where one of his footmen went to spend three or four days with him, and where he spent money profusely and recklessly. In conclusion it was added that the Legate of Ravenna, having sent for him, as he got into his carriage, he was holding in his hand a paper that he pointed to with a laugh, as if to say —

"I've only got to make myself known!"

But I was not satisfied by these vague, general reports; I wanted witnesses who had seen with their own eyes and heard with their own ears; and I succeeded in discovering them.

Not to speak of the sisters Bandini, who related what happened in the bosom of the families into which they were admitted as confidential servants, or of Count Borghi, who quoted in support of his theory his careful perusal of certain papers immensely in my favour, this is how the Signore Giovanni-Maria Valla, of Brisighella, spoke on the subject —

"It is more than fifty years since I was enrolled in the Country Militia. Shortly afterwards, when I had already risen to the rank of Corporal, I was put in charge of a stranger called by the title of Comte, whom the constables had taken up in the neighbourhood of the Convent of St. Bernard. I did not know the man, who was well-made and rather stout, with a reddish-brown complexion.

"It was said that the order for his arrest came from Ravenna; but I know nothing about the reason for it nor anything else about him, except that a few days later we gave him up again to the Cardinal's Swiss guards, who took him away in his carriage. As for Lorenzo Chiappini, I knew him very well, having seen him several times at Brisighella, where he used to come to play football, and I remember having heard it said that he had given up his post because he had got a great lot of money for exchanging his boy for the girl of a rich nobleman."

And again, this is what the Signore Giuseppe Guezzani, of the same town, said —

"My business has always been that of a barber, and I always served the Fathers of St. Bernard until they were suppressed. It is about fifty years since I used occasionally to shave a stranger living with them, who passed for a great

French nobleman. I was left in ignorance as to who he was or why he was there. Afterwards I heard that he had been arrested, but I was never told the reason. He was rather stout, of good height, and had a brownish complexion with a red and pimply nose. I remember, too, that he had very fine legs."

And this is the account of the Signore Giuseppe Tondini, another inhabitant of the town—

"About fifty years ago a foreign nobleman was living for some days in the convent of St. Bernard then existing in this town of Brisighella. I don't know to what nation he belonged, and I don't remember him well enough to describe him; but I think he was about the average height and rather stout. It was reported afterwards that he had been arrested."

Then there is the story of the Signore Ludovichetti, a lawyer living at Ravenna—

"Some length of time before the changes in this province —I can't tell the exact date, but it was certainly during the time I was practising in the Criminal Court of that Legation, which was from 1768 to 1793—being about one o'clock one day in the said Court, I heard that a foreign nobleman of exalted rank had been arrested, and was being brought to our prison under an escort of soldiers. His Eminence, being told of his arrival, had him at once brought before him. Moved by curiosity, I left my office and went into the Cardinal-Legate's room, and there I saw that when this nobleman appeared, his Eminence went forward to meet him, embraced him, and led him into his own apartments. A good half-hour later, having gone back to my work, I heard the carriage; and looking out of the window, I saw the said nobleman get into it, and it crossed the square in the direction of the Adrian Gate by which it had entered. I don't know who he was or where he came from, nor do I know

99

where or why he was arrested. But he was said to be a great French personage."

Having heard these eye-witnesses, let us listen to others whose reputations make them worthy of full belief.

Let us listen to the Signore Domenico della Valle, Secretary to the parish of Brisighella—

"Though very intimate with one of the Fathers of St. Bernard, I never heard him say a word about the exchange in question. But I can vouch for the fact that before 1790 I had heard the fact much talked about by several persons, and especially by the late Maestro don Giovanni-Batista Tondini, who seemed to know all about it. He told me that the thing had taken place about fifty years ago in the little town of Modigliana between a great French nobleman living in the Pretorial Palace, who had exchanged his daughter for the son of a certain Chiappini, then a constable, and whom I knew very well later on when he used to come to Brisighella to play football as an amateur. About twenty-five years ago I again saw, in the piazza of the Grand Duke, the said Chiappini, who talked for a long time with the late Cesare Bandini of Veriolo, who was with me. When that gentleman came back to me, I said to him: 'You have been talking to a man I know to have exchanged his boy for the daughter of a great French nobleman.' And Bandini replied, 'Yes, that's the man, and we were talking privately about that business.'

"I can say for certain that Chiappini was well dressed then, and I was told he was in easy circumstances, and had no need to follow his original occupation.

"After the suppression of the monastery of St. Bernard, I was employed in helping to make an inventory of papers and effects belonging to it. As I could speak French, they made me read two letters written in that language. They were addressed to the Father Abbot, signed L. C. Joinville, and bore the date of 1773; but I can't remember what day or what month.

"In the first, written from Modigliana, there were thanks to that Father for having allowed him to take refuge in his convent; and in the second, written from Ravenna, he informed him that he had been set at liberty after having been arrested and taken to that town, and thanked him for all the attention he had shown him. These letters were written in a running and uneven hand; if I could see another written by the same person I should probably recognize it.

"The brothers of St. Bernard had themselves told me that the Count was taken up one morning when he had gone out for a walk with a book; and they added that their Abbot, looking upon this arrest as a violation of a sacred sanctuary, had been to Ravenna to lodge a complaint, and had obtained satisfaction.

"There was nothing entered in the inventory but the title-deeds of the capital and interest of the convent; the letters and other papers were left as being of no use; no one looked after them, and I don't know if they are still in existence."

Now let us hear Don Gaspare Perelli, Canon at Ravenna —

"I can perfectly well remember, about forty-three years ago, hearing some one say to my father, who was Governor of Brisighella, that some years earlier a prince in disguise, who was stopping in that part of the country, had exchanged his daughter for the son of a constable, and that this had taken place in the neighbourhood of Brisighella, though I can't remember the name of the place itself. My father often told this story at table, and in the presence of my mother, Angela Forchini; and then they would inveigh against the cruelty of so changing a girl of high rank for a boy of low condition."

Finally, let us hear the Signore Marco Maresta, chief custom-house officer in that same town of Ravenna—

"It is a long time ago, and I couldn't swear to the exact date, that several people told me that at Faenza, or, as they said later, at Modigliana, there had taken place an exchange of the daughter of a great nobleman for a boy of low condition whose father had received a large sum, and that this exchange had been arranged beforehand when the two wives were about to be confined. I can't remember the name of the nobleman nor that of the base man who accepted his offer, nor even that of the people who told me about it; but I did hear that the first was a Frenchman."

With so many proofs at my command, I thought the time had come to push on my case. To procure greater expedition, I thought of another innocent stratagem.

From Ravenna, whither I had gone so that I could not be suspected of complicity with my judges, I wrote a letter to the Count Borghi, in which I pretended to have been informed that, my friends having discovered my true family in France, not one of my relations was left but a nun living at Bordeaux, who would welcome me with the greatest delight if I could succeed in proving to her the truth of the exchange, etc.

Quite beside himself, that gentleman hastened to announce this piece of good news to the Bishop of Faenza, came to Ravenna to congratulate me, and added to what he had already told me that the Count and Countess Borghi, his informants, though held in the highest esteem, were both of a very giddy and thoughtless disposition; that the last-named used to remit to the former doorkeeper an annual pension sent by the Comte Joinville for my education, and that the Grand Duke Leopold had shown me great favour.

"Do you suppose," he said, "that except for that, that Prince would have been so deeply interested in you? Do you suppose he would have taken so much trouble or done so much for such a miserable wretch as Chiappini, etc.?"

Having promised me that he would mention all this in his deposition, he started for home, where he set everything going. His great eagerness made me alter my opinion of him; I could not believe that he still wished to conceal from me any helpful letters he might possess, and thenceforth my belief was that he had originally handed them all over to my supposed brother, with whom I knew he had had some communication.

Not to be behindhand with his fervour, I made haste to engage as my lawyer the Signore Jérôme Bellenghi, in order to obtain from the Episcopal Tribunal sitting at Faenza the proper rectification of my baptismal certificate; and this tribunal, on its side, nominated the Count Carlo Bandini to fill the office of proxy as representative of the Comte and Comtesse de Joinville, not present.

My so-called brother, Tomaso Chiappini, was assigned me as my representative, but, though twice summoned, refused to appear.

After the aforesaid witnesses had made their attestations, they were cross-examined, and their answers were in strict accordance with their original accounts.

My counsel having argued his case, his opponent argued his and raised every difficulty possible.

The Tribunal, having, after mature consideration, come to the conclusion that the attestation of the deceased jailer, far from being improbable, had been confirmed and verified by

a large number of other evidence, presumptions and conjectures, gave, on the 29th of May, 1824, a verdict entirely in my favour; and when the proper time for appealing against it was over, no objection having been raised, the Registrar, under this warrant, proceeded to carry out the definitive rectification of my birth certificate, and declared me to be the *daughter of the husband and wife, M. le Comte Louis, and Madame la Comtesse N. de Joinville.* (French.)
[5]

[147]
[148]

IV

Fresh Investigations—Count Borghi's Letters—The Baths of Lucca—
Intimacy of the Duke of Orleans and the Marchioness of B.—Loan
—The Chevalier Montara—Letter to the Duc de Bourbon—
Various Publications—The Lawyer Courtilly—Archives of
Genoa—Conduct of the Governor—Tomaso Chiappini's Libel—
Refusal of the Printers—Vain Attempts—The Bishop of Faenza—
Letter from the Cape of Good Hope.

One important fact had been argued and settled, namely, that of my substitution; and thenceforth it would be incontestable that my parents were the Comte and Comtesse de Joinville, and French. But who were this couple, and where were they? The uncertainty about this was insupportable to me now, and I was inspired with fresh courage to renew the struggle.

Greatly wishing, if possible, to discover the nurse who had suckled the jailer's son, I had notices put up in several towns that a large reward would be given to any one who could give me news of her.

I wrote about this matter to Count Borghi, and at the same time reproached him somewhat for having omitted, on examination, to add to his first declaration what he had come to Ravenna to tell me.

This was his answer—

"HONOURED LADY,

"It is enough for me that you are pleased with what I have done, and if you keep your goodwill for me, my delight will be complete.

"You must never doubt of our everlasting remembrance of you, whom we love and esteem for your rare and excellent qualities. I have heard how much vexed you were by the ignorance of the copyists; I could not have believed they could be so stupid and illiterate; but the Bishop will have all that remedied.

"All these unlooked-for difficulties must have worried you and delay our progress still more; I am truly sorry for it, and if I could have foreseen it, I would have offered to make the copies myself.

"During my examination I answered every question put to me, and I wanted to add what I told you at Ravenna; but I was told that, as that could not strengthen my deposition, it was useless to include it in the case. I did not fail to ask the sisters Bandini if they had not still got some remains of the correspondence between the Countess Camilla and the Comte de Joinville, but they always answered that they had absolutely nothing left of it.

"And that must be true; for if they possessed any of your parents' letters they would have thought of making something out of them to relieve their poverty.

"Your nurse at Modigliana was the mother of a woman who is still alive; as to that of the exchanged boy, no one has been able to give me news of her; and prudence would have prevented the author of so atrocious a crime from choosing her about here, and also from leaving any trace of the direction in which the Comtesse de Joinville, with her attendants, went.

"I will go to Modigliana shortly, where I will make it my duty to make every possible inquiry, as you desire; but I greatly fear they will be fruitless, like those of so many others whom you employed before me, amongst whom was the Signore Ragazzini, who took immense trouble.

"I think I have now answered all the questions in your letter, which I received from your courier, from whom we heard, to our great delight, that you and your beloved Edward, to whom we send our best love, are in perfect health. Your friend[6] swears an eternal affection for you; she joins with me in wishing you the greatest success and a full recovery of your sacred rights.

"Believe, honoured lady, that my protestations of respect and attachment could not be more sincere; and I can flatter myself that, from the moment I made your personal acquaintance, I was, and shall always be, proud to be your humble and devoted servant, as well as your very affectionate friend.

"NICHOLAS BORGHI-BIANCOLI."

After so much anxiety, worry and fatigue, I felt the greatest need of rest, and my dear Marchioness of B. having most luckily told me that she was at the baths of Lucca, I

106

hastened to throw myself into her loving arms there.

She told me that, about six weeks after my going to Paris, she had written the *Duke of Orleans* a second letter of introduction for me, and said that she had been much surprised that *that Prince* had not acknowledged its receipt, and had not even taken the trouble to thank her for the news she had given him of her daughter's marriage to Lord S.

For it is as well to know that, during the time of their exile, the *Duke and his two brothers*[7] had received from Mr. C., the Marchioness's father, an annual pension of £200 and permi to dine with him as often as they pleased.

THE DUKE OF ORLEANS

The Marquess of B. had given them a similar invitation, and had offered them the use of a country house a short distance from London.

The Duc de Montpensier, filled with gratitude, was so greatly attached to him that he had himself carried to him just before his death, saying that he must go to give an eternal farewell to his best friend.

This Prince having died of consumption at the age of thirty-two, the unfortunate Comte de Beaujolais, already attacked by the same disease, was taken by his *elder brother* to a milder climate, and died at Malta during his twenty-eighth year.

On his return to England, the present Duke applied once more to Mr. C. and the Marquess of B. and obtained fresh favours and assistance, to supply, as he said, the needs of his mother and *sister*.

A short time after the Restoration, the Marchioness being in Paris, he went to see her, thanked her for all her good offices, vowed eternal gratitude to her and pressed her to go to spend a few days at Neuilly. Her health prevented her from yielding to his gracious entreaties or those of the Duchess, who also showed her great kindness; but from that time there began a very friendly and almost fraternal correspondence between the Duke and my friend, which was interrupted only by the sending of the letter concerning me.

I could easily explain to my friend the cause of this silence, by telling her of all that had happened since I had had the happiness of seeing her.

The enormous expenses I had incurred had exhausted my funds, and I asked her to be so good as to advance me something.

At first she refused, pleading that her intimacy with the Duke would not allow her to provide weapons against him; but my arguments, and still more her own love for me, little by little convinced her, and she ended by lending me the sum I needed.

With scrupulous delicacy she informed my adversary of

109

this, assuring him that it was solely to give me the power of paying off my old debts and not with the intention of helping me to make war on him.

Instead of a direct answer to so expansive a confidence, a thousand tortuous ways were taken to convince my friend that my claims were nothing but a tissue of lies, and everything possible was done to deprive me of her affection.

But her never-failing answer was: "Let her ideas be true or false, my heart will always be with one whom I love like another self."

As soon as I had somewhat recovered, I went to Genoa, so as to be more within reach of news from France, whither I had made up my mind to send a certain Chevalier Montara whom a lady in Lucca had described as being a very clever man. I gave him my instructions and £300 sterling, for the journey as well as for the investigations he would have to make, and ordered him to submit the whole thing to his Majesty Louis XVIII.

His first letters were very encouraging, and they came pretty frequently; soon they became rarer and rarer; he tried to arouse fears in me; he pleaded serious illness, squandered my money, and, in fact, did nothing for me.

About this time, I was reminded that the Duc de Bourbon-Condé, during his misfortunes, had received much civility from Lord Newborough's relations. Delighted at this reminiscence, I thought I might take the liberty of writing a very respectful and touching letter to His Highness, begging him to give me his advice.

My letter was delivered, opened, and having been looked at, was ignominiously returned to the person who had undertaken to take it.

The secretary who gave it back to him censured my

action, accused me of audacity, and treated my business as a chimerical delusion.

After this disappointment I was advised to have recourse to Madame la Dauphine.

A literary man of high reputation undertook to draw up my petition after the most proper fashion; but when he came to read it to me, I must confess that it seemed to me far from likely to convince any one of the truth, especially at a time so fertile in impostors.

Despite the doubts which I thought might be caused by my ignorance of a language that was still almost unknown to me, I decided to have it presented by a gentleman residing in Paris, who, at the end of three weeks wrote that he must not again be given such commissions; that he had been asked several questions he could not answer, and that he had found himself, without any manner of doubt, under the special observance of the police.

This fresh worry was all the more trying since my stay in Genoa was disturbed by a multitude of other anxieties.

Not content with distributing copies of the judgment given at Faenza, I had an article inserted in a newspaper[8] containing a summary of my case, in which I asked for fresh information concerning my father and mother, whom I designated only by the initial J.

No one could believe that they were simply nobles; everybody was whispering august names; but as the Orleans family was allied with all the reigning families of Italy, fear seized upon all hearts and closed all lips.

Only one man made his appearance: a former magistrate who had known old Chiappini well.

As a matter of fact, his evidence would have been much more useful to me before the verdict given in my favour, but at least it will serve to confirm it. Let us listen to it.

"I, the undersigned, certify and declare what follows, on my soul and conscience—

"In the year 1808, having sent in my resignation of the post of substitute of the Attorney-General in the Criminal Court of the department called that of the Apennines, I retired to Florence, where I lived until the month of April 1813, the date of my departure for Rome. At the beginning of my residence in the first of these two towns, I made the acquaintance of Lorenzo Chiappini, with whom I sometimes dined at the house of the doctor, Pietro Salvi. In 1810, I met him, with other Florentines, in the immense house of the old Chartreuse, where, like me, he had hired rooms to spend the summer in. The more we saw of each other the more intimate and familiar became our intercourse, especially on his side.

"Very soon he told me the most minute details of a journey he had made to London to see one of his daughters, married, he said, to a rich English lord who had fallen in love with her on hearing her sing in a theatre.

"He could not say enough about the splendour of his son-in-law's house, nor of the welcome he had received there; told me some coarse stories about Great Britain; described the manners of the inhabitants; constantly repeated that all his happiness lay in that darling daughter, and assured me that he would give the world to procure the pleasure of seeing her again.

"The next year he was attacked by some slight malady, and one day, as I went to see him pretty frequently, he confessed to me that he had a great burden on his conscience. I tried in vain to make him listen to some words of comfort; nothing could cure his melancholy.

"Another time, the talk having turned on the same subject, I said that if he had not been guilty of theft—a sin God does not pardon without restitution—all else could be expiated by repentance. At that he made a clean breast of everything, and confided to me that, having been in his youth keeper of the prisons at Modigliana, he exchanged his firstborn son for the daughter of a foreign nobleman, and that it was that daughter who was married in London, and that he should feel never-ending regret for so having helped to deprive her of her birthright.

"Having strongly advised him to reveal such a secret to his generous benefactress, who must most certainly rejoice over it because of the honour and profit it would bring her, he said that he had already thought of doing so, and only wanted to avoid any sort of fuss during his life; but he should manage so that everything should be discovered after his death. He added that this seemed sufficient reparation due to the lady, considering her present condition of grandeur and opulence.

"He talked after the same fashion to me on several other occasions, and I always found him fixed in that resolve.

"This is what I heard from Chiappini's own lips, and I am prepared to confirm it, if necessary, legally and by oath.

"In testimony whereof,

"Louis Courtilly,

"Lawyer."

This very clear and precise deposition was far from compensating me for all the disagreeables brought upon me by my harmless advertisements.

Researches made in the Public Archives of the town I was living in brought to light almost nothing about the year 1773; the Keeper of the Records declared that the books relating to that period had been put together in a place I must not enter without special permission, and where, he told me, memorandums of great importance were kept.

But it was impossible to get anything out of the Governor, who was my sworn enemy.

The day after the appearance of my article he had severely reprimanded the journalist I had employed.

He often gave balls, concerts and entertainments of all kinds, to which all the English ladies, from those of high rank down to the wives of the smallest tradespeople, were invited; I alone was deprived of this *immense honour*.

One day he went so far as to express to my banker the greatest desire for my speedy departure. "I am ordered," he said, "to keep the strictest watch over her."

My banker replying that he could not understand the reason of it, since all I was doing was in order to discover a Comte and Comtesse Joinville—

"Yes," said this officious governor; "but it isn't very easy to prove that this Count and Countess are no other than the former Duke and Duchess of Chartres?"

But that was not all.

Fifteen days after the appearance of my article in the *Gazetta di Genova*, my ex-brother, the advocate Chiappini, sent me by post a so-called answer he had had put into the public papers, boasting of having obtained the permission of the Government. Adorned with all the flowers of speech an infamous pen could indite, such a libel was well worthy of its author.

Although my reputation stood immeasurably high above his insults, at first I wanted to answer them.

The first printer I spoke to refused his services, under the pretext that he had received orders in the matter; I had successive recourse to several others, who all likewise put me off. Not only at Genoa, but at Florence, Bologna and Alessandria—everywhere they had been threatened with severe penalties in case of disobedience.

Tomaso Chiappini had not confined himself to spreading atrocious calumnies against me; I heard that he was accusing my witnesses of imposture, and that several of them, alarmed by the sinister rumours he circulated, and believing themselves irretrievably ruined, were cursing me and declaring that I had involved them in the greatest trouble.

Amongst these was the Count Borghi, who henceforth became once more my enemy.

The whole country was topsy-turvy; but all these intrigues, all these diabolical plots fell to the ground.

I wrote to the Bishop of Faenza, who could not get over his astonishment, but exhorted me to suspend judgment on the persons whose perfidious inconstancy I was denouncing, and assured me that the truth was too well established for anything henceforth to shake it.

His letter, which I carefully treasure, is dated July 20, 1826.

If that of this venerable prelate, illustrious by his learning and formerly Patriarch of Venice, was flattering and an honour, another, which I received from the Cape of Good Hope, was as vile and filthy.

It can easily be guessed it was the work of that other Chiappini to whom Lord Newborough had shown so much kindness.

The most malignant rage was manifest through the whole of it, beneath the hideous hues of expressions as indescribably ignoble as they were ridiculous.

To do full justice to it, it would doubtless be enough to let it be seen as it is; but I should fear to disgust my readers.

V

I go to Nice—Rudeness of the Governor—Letter from Alquier-Caze —My Precautions—Demands, and Remittances—Second Journey to Paris—Conversation—A Gouty Colonel—Expenses—Return to Nice—Letters from my Husband—His Arrival—That of the Marchioness of B.—A Transient Happiness.

Being so ill-treated at Genoa, and also wishing to be still nearer to France, in the month of September 1825, with my son, his tutor and my servants, I left and went to live in a country house I had rented near the gates of Nice, where I was unlucky enough to come across a governor still stiffer and ruder than that of the town I had just left.

But what could so many unjust proceedings do but confirm me still more in the justice of my high claims! For it was easy enough for me to see that they were dictated by a powerful hand, and I could not believe that that kind of enemy would fight mere phantoms.

A little before this I had received a letter from Paris, written by a certain Alquier-Caze, who introduced himself and offered me his services.

"I have been well posted up in the case," he wrote; "I know its delicacy, I see its difficulties; but I don't feel any qualms about undertaking it; and I even count on a speedy success if you will deign to honour me with your complete confidence."

Afraid of falling again into the hands of a rogue, I sent him a very guarded and cautious letter; but he was not at all put out by it, and replied in these terms—

"Madame la Baronne, the position you are in is such as to cause you great anxiety. The importance of the matter that fills your mind; the uncertainty of its issue; the base machinations that perfidy has employed against you; the kind of fatality that seems to pursue you, all combine to give birth to endless doubts and apprehensions. But, believe me, Madame, I feel the strongest conviction that, by my hands, Heaven will give you the final victory over your enemies. Yes, that victory will be my work. Up to now you have been deceived; up to now I have met with nothing but ingratitude for my services; Fate keeps in reserve for each of us an equally pleasant event; for you, that of seeing your confidence justified by my vigorous efforts; for me, that of meeting at last with a noble expression of gratitude. No, the soul of a Catalan is not an ordinary soul, as the future will prove to you better than anything I could say," etc.

The confident warmth of this shook me. I had some inquiries made about him, and as I was told he was a young lawyer of good repute, bold and clever, I decided to confide my documents to him.

He wrote soon, declaring that he had already made some valuable discoveries, intimating at the same time that the

117

lure of gain was absolutely necessary for obtaining good evidence.

I at once set about sending off a considerable sum to him, which was but the prelude to the many other such disbursements the necessity of which he was continually urging.

This had gone on for several months, when, some weeks after my arrival at Nice, I received a fresh letter from Caze, telling me that he was beginning the attack at the reopening of the Courts; that he greatly wished to confer with me beforehand, and urging me so strongly to come to Paris before the 1st of November, that I set out at once, taking with me my dear son and his tutor.

In spite of all the haste we made, we could not manage to arrive before the 2nd of November. I took a suite of rooms in a large hotel in the Place Vendôme, and not till two days later did I receive the first visit of my *assiduous* lawyer.

Compliments exchanged, this represents the substance of what passed between us—

"Have you got your husband's authority, madame?" "No, monsieur." "But that is a document without which we can do nothing." "You ought to have warned me of that six months ago." "I most sincerely beg your pardon for not having thought of it." "It is very annoying to have taken so long and expensive a journey uselessly." "Far from being useless, it was indispensable." "I don't see why." "Wasn't it necessary for us to arrange together what it would be best to attempt so as to ensure complete success?"

"That could have been done by writing, or after I had been furnished with the power-of-attorney."

"Yes; but I was longing to tell you in person what I could not confide to paper."

"What are these very important communications, then?" "I have succeeded in discovering that the very year of the exchange the Duc de Chartres, your father, was staying at Berne, under the name of the Comte de Joinville, in an inn the then landlady of which is still alive; and where he scandalized everybody by his profligate conduct. I believe I can get a certification of this from the local authorities. Another of my agents has informed me that the Marquise de Boucherolles, an old friend of your mother's, testifies that that Princess was on bad terms with her supposed son, and often made mysterious remarks that are in perfect agreement with the facts of the case.

"The same agent spoke to me of a certain M. d'Echouards, who knows of the testimony of the late Madame Cambise to the effect that, on her death-bed, the Dowager suffered greatly from a troubled conscience. He told me, too, that the late mother-in-law of the Comte de Saillan was one of the travelling-party in 1773. Moreover, on this point I have three witnesses *de visu*, and am just about to procure three more still living." "Will you be so very kind as to introduce them to me?" "Most willingly; but I shall still need a little more money to give them enough courage. That's by far the best card to play, especially in Paris."

Bewitched by his talk and his protestations, I opened my purse, and my poor pennies disappeared into that of my artful juggler, who, the next day, appeared once more, bringing with him a gouty old Colonel, who, almost before he got into the room, addressed me in the following words —

"As I am well acquainted with the family of the Baron de Sternberg, I want to help you as much as I possibly can. The judgments of men being always doubtful, you may perhaps fail in obtaining the justice you seem to expect from legal tribunals; but it would be quite easy for you, through

119

my intervention, to arrive at a satisfactory settlement."

Astonished at such a speech, I promptly exclaimed: "No, no; I would never consent to submit to such a disgrace."

The Colonel replied—

"Still, madame, the plan I want to propose to you would undoubtedly be the wisest and the most advantageous for you. Will you live long enough to see the end of such a case? And how do you know that your children would have any desire to go on with it?"

To this my answer was still more concise, being couched in three words: "All or nothing!"

I left the room as soon as they were uttered, and declined to see my gouty old friend again, believing him to be a spy sent from my adversary.

Vainly I waited for the appearance of M. Alquier's promised witnesses; there were always fresh excuses on his part, and renewed requests for money, which I was simple enough to grant. In less than a fortnight I had spent more than three thousand crowns.

Weary of such expenses and delays, I longed to return to Nice, where I arrived towards the end of the autumn. I had written to my husband, who, during the winter, sent me his very disappointing opinion. Instead of authorizing me to go to law, he advised attempting to come to some arrangement.

I seized my pen at once to tell him shortly that, desiring to die as I had lived, I could not compromise my honour.

Some months after, I received a second letter, in which he told me that, on the advice of our friend, Admiral Krusenstern,[9] he was coming to me, so as to endeavour to end the business in the best way possible.

He arrived towards the end of October, having stopped some time in Paris to make fresh investigations. While allowing that I had excellent grounds and very favourable chances, his constant refrain was: "We must try for an arrangement"; while mine was a vexed and endless repetition of: "All or nothing."

His arrival was shortly followed by that of the Marchioness of B., who came from Lausanne.

She told me that *the Duke of Orleans*, while visiting that town, had not condescended even to ask news of her; adding that she quite understood that I was the innocent cause of this base ingratitude.

The house she took at Nice being next door to mine, we saw each other constantly; in fact, we were always together, and I can assert that that winter was the happiest time in my wretched existence; though even then I could not fully enjoy its consolations, because of my firm conviction that they would speedily change to bitter sufferings.

My presentiments were but too well verified; my friend, for her part, was obliged to go back to London, while the Baron, on his, announced his positive intention to send Edward to a public school!

VI

My Stay at Geneva—Correspondence of Alquier-Caze—M. Sparifico
—Payment of the Lawyers—An Unlucky Meeting—Weakening
of my Health—My Husband's Exhortations—His Arrival with
Driver-Cooper—Fatal Agreement—My Son's Tutor.

In the middle of the year 1827, soon after the departure of
my friend, we transported our household goods to Geneva,
where was the school my husband had chosen for our
young son; and his first care on our arrival was the
carrying out of his barbarous plan.

Unable to make up my mind quite to lose sight of the dear
child who, since his birth, had never left me, I hired a house
close to his. I was able to go to see him every day, to lavish
love upon him, and he himself came to see me twice a week
and spent the whole of Sunday with me.

I used to invite several of his school-fellows for the
evening, providing all sorts of refreshments for them, and
letting them amuse themselves just as they pleased; and
their childish games were a real relaxation to me.

Moreover, my dear Marchioness of B. had kindly given me
several agreeable introductions, so that in my new home I
found something of the pleasure I had enjoyed at Nice.

But this new tranquillity could not last.

For some time past I had noticed that d'Alquier-Caze's
communications were neither so frequent nor so hopeful as
they had been. Having mentioned this to him, he answered
me by a lengthy enumeration of his supposed services.
Another time he wrote that he was going to Nancy to
question an old person he had been told of from whose
evidence he expected the happiest results.

On another occasion he gave me an account of a
conversation he professed to have had with a Minister of his

most Christian Majesty.

"The first attempt was to frighten me," he said; "but my determined aspect speedily destroyed all hope of succeeding in that. Then discouragement was tried; I made a suitable reply. Every possible way of trying to make me speak was used; but I steadily kept myself within the limits of a wise discretion. *'What do you want?'* I was asked. My answer was yours: *'All or nothing.' 'You'll ruin yourself.' 'I shall do my duty.' 'You had better give up such a chimerical business.' 'I possess the confidence of milady, and I cannot betray it.' 'You will never succeed.' 'We shall.' 'Every one regards your claims with supreme contempt.' 'That's impossible!' 'They can't conceive on what you found them.' 'Do you allow that the exchange took place?' 'Yes.' 'Then all that I have to do now is to prove the identity of its perpetrator with the too notorious Orleans.' 'Prove even its likelihood, if you can.' 'I shall prove its reality.' 'How?' 'We shall have writings and witnesses.' 'Well, we shall always be pleased to see you.' 'I shall come again.'* etc."

Far from satisfied with all this talk, I constantly complained that, since the verdict given at Faenza, I had spent a great deal of money and was still about where I was then. To combat my reproaches he conceived the idea of writing me the extraordinary letter here given—

"You are angry with me, dear milady, are you not? You are both right and wrong. You are right, because in your situation nothing could be more natural than impatience; and wrong, because I am to be excused on account of all the trouble I am taking.

"There is a question I am about to submit to you, and to which you must give a definite answer.

"Certain proposals, in the form of advice, have been made to me in your interest. Would you be disposed—

123

yes or no—to come to an arrangement if its terms were considerable pecuniary advantages to yourself? Please let me know at once. I won't say more to-day, but that everything is going on well. Believe me, etc."

What more was wanted to open my eyes and let me clearly see the crafty duplicity of my ill-advised rascal, who up to now had so piqued himself on the nobility of his sentiments?

Knowing in Paris a certain M. Sparifico, I begged him to tell me of some lawyer famous for his ability and still more for his integrity.

First he mentioned several, who, he said, dared not undertake my defence; and then he named others whom I knew to be devoted to my mortal enemy.

I was so disgusted with all these obstacles that I almost made up my mind to give up everything.

The Baron being obliged to go to the capital of France on his own affairs, I requested him to recover all the papers in Alquier-Caze's possession, which he endeavoured to do; but could not manage till he had paid 200 francs to Maître Hennequin for a memorandum I had never seen; 550 francs to Maître Plé for work of which I had never heard, and 1000 francs to Caze himself for having cheated me out of many times as much.

About this time a certain Henry Driver-Cooper, who, after ruining his creditors in England, had taken refuge on the Continent so as to increase his iniquitous fortune, had just exchanged his modest designation of hop-merchant for the pompous title of jurisconsult, which he thought he had the right to share with Maître Dupin, considering that he had entrusted to him the celebrated Stacpoole case;[10] wherefore he considered that he also ought to share in the glory of its success; since, without him, Maître Dupin would not have intervened. He had his *Doctor's Diploma* printed on his visiting-cards, and went from house to house boasting of his triumph.

But he took good care not to add that Maître Dupin himself, thinking but little of his services, had reduced the fee he claimed by a thirty-second!

After this blow the disconsolate hop-merchant, or, if you like, the saddened jurisconsult, was on the look-out for a favourable opportunity. He owned in the neighbourhood of Paris a so-called *château*, which he had bought in better days, and he was trying to find an obliging tenant who would pay him a big rent for it while still leaving him in possession and even keeping him during the whole duration of the lease.

I was to be this compassionate person; he had foreseen it from the moment that he had first chanced to meet my husband, whom by dexterous suggestions he drew into his net, and negotiations were entered into.

Meanwhile, the damp climate of Geneva having given me a very bad cold, which, as usual, had at once settled on my chest, my friends advised me to take a house in the country where I could breathe more healthy air. I had chosen one, called Coligny, looking over the lake and magnificently situated, when the Baron, writing to me about his *lucky discovery*, asked my opinion of it.

In spite of his youth, my dear son begged me not to forget how many times I had allowed myself to be caught in the snares of impostors. In consequence I answered evasively, and principally to tell my husband of my resolve to change my house.

I soon received a second letter in which he implored me

not to carry out my intention, explained still more fully the conditions laid down by my *deliverer*, and told me that one of them was that I must live in his house during the whole course of the trial.

This time my answer was decided.

"I will consent," I said, "to combine with your agent in pecuniary matters if he will pay half the costs and undertake to push on the business briskly. As to the plan for my living in his house, you may give that up at once; for I intend to take the one I have in view here from to-morrow, and nothing will induce me to leave my dear Edward."

In fact, I signed the agreement and moved to Coligny.

I was hardly settled there when I had a third letter from the Baron, expressing very great displeasure and even reproving me in a way. He spoke enthusiastically of Cooper, extolling his courtesy, enlarging on his ability, and endeavouring above all to convince me that if I did not take advantage of his generous offer I might give up all my hopes; that I should not find any French *avocat* willing to fight against the powerful Colossus, reputed the first Prince of the Royal Blood, and that the great benefit to my son claimed the sacrifice, however painful to my heart, of a separation destined to procure for him the most brilliant of futures.

That last argument moved and shook me; it was so cleverly put that I consented to see our charlatan. But the clever swindler, not wishing to make it seem that he had come on his own initiative to see me in Switzerland, got a model of the flattering invitation I was to give him sent to me.

My exact copy having reached him, he and my husband arrived.

He left no stone unturned to dazzle our eyes with his cunning promises, and, as soon as he believed us both well prepared, he persuaded us to go to the house of Voltaire at Ferney.

"It shall be on the very table at which the great man wrote his immortal works that our agreement shall be signed; his shade shall preside there, and his presence be the pledge of the most glorious success."

It was pure farce, I own, but what is easier than to inflame minds already under the spell? Could we haggle when the grandeurs and riches we had a right to claim were, so to speak, at our discretion?

Cooper was able to take advantage of our weakness in the most infamous fashion.

Sitting unmoved in this castle-in-the-air of his own building, caring for nothing but other people's money, he made us affix our signatures to two deeds, the outcome of his crafty cupidity.

By the first he appointed himself my steward; as such he was, during the whole course of the trial, to lodge and keep me; to furnish me with horses, carriages, and servants, in return for an annual payment of 25,000 francs, payable in advance.

Having made his calculations correctly, by the second, which he had taken care to bring ready drawn-up and in French so uncouth that it was difficult to understand it, he created himself the absolute dispenser of larger sums.

He was to proceed with the business which was my principal object *if he thought fit, and in the way he thought best.* The costs were to be divided, and, in the case of success, the profits also.

"Perhaps you have not by you the sum you ought to pay

me. Well, give me bills."

And so I did to the amount of £1,150 sterling.

After this delightful expedition, he was ready to return to Paris, begging me to follow quickly.

Although at school my son had all the necessary masters, I had up to now kept on his tutor, called Ragazzini, a native of Tredozzio, who had been recommended to me at Florence as a clever man, and had taken some trouble in the Faenza business.

I wished to discharge him at this time in consequence of many defects he could no longer keep hidden; but Cooper and the Baron were against it, saying that the man, knowing Italy perfectly, might be of the greatest use to us; so, though very reluctantly, I gave way to their urgent representations; and it was arranged that he was to accompany me and my husband.

VII

Painful Separation—Arrival at Bellevue—Powers given to Cooper—His Swindling—The Ills he made me suffer—Fresh Attempts of Alquier-Caze—Distraint on my Effects—My Move to the Hôtel Britannique—Letters from my Husband and my Son—My Grief and my Resolves.

Immediately after Cooper's departure I began to prepare. The owner of Coligny was inexorable; I had to pay him the whole year's rent.

But this loss was very small compared with another much greater one. It would be vain to try to describe how my maternal heart was torn, when I thought I was forsaking my dear son. How difficult it was, what restraint I had to use, what efforts to make, not to break down when the dear boy asked me with sorrowful and almost prophetic voice: "Maman, Maman, what are you going to do?"

And all I could say in answer was: "My darling, I am going to work for the good of you and your dear brothers."

Before the fatal day he spent two with me, and his loving caresses were sweet but incurable wounds to my soul.

No—I will not attempt to describe that cruel parting; I will not speak of it. I will only say that, absorbed in my own thoughts, despite the numerous requests to do so, I could not bear once to look at the sublime and delightful beauties of nature, which had always had so great a charm for me.

After a journey of four days we passed through Paris, and arrived at Bellevue near Meudon.

One of the chief reasons that had induced me to go to the scene of action was the inclination my husband and his confidant had shown to try the plan of compromise with my adversary; and I was quite resolved to make an eternal protest against that kind of baseness. But once on the spot, I thought there was nothing to fear. Deeds, papers, documents, got together with difficulty by my constant care —all were handed over without misgiving, and the full powers demanded by Cooper at once given him.

But that was not enough; he must seize my whole fortune. My income was now reduced to £1,700 sterling a year; he had already taken £1000 for the rent of the house; but he could not be satisfied till he got hold of the £700 I still had to dispose of.

To this end, he got together some infamous assistants, with whom he worked upon the Baron's mind with shameless cunning, and they came all together to propose my giving the rogue fresh powers to raise my funds in England, under pretext of the enormous expenses my case would entail.

No more powerful motive could have been offered me; after a few short explanations, I signed a paper, which I had not even been asked to read.

So now Cooper was absolute master of my property; there was nothing more for him to ask for: he had got it all.

And now the important trial for which I had already made such great sacrifices would surely make mighty strides towards the desired event?

By no means; Cooper isn't even giving it a thought; anyhow there is nothing to prove that he is. But he is always talking to me in a hopeful strain, so important is it to him to keep his post as director of a sham piece of work which, without care or trouble, ought to bring him in 45,000 francs a year!

But the agreement as to rent and stewardship was very ill carried out; for several weeks carriage, horses, servants could not be found; our rooms lacked the most necessary pieces of furniture, and my table displayed such parsimony that I should infallibly have died of hunger if I had not taken care to get in from outside something to live upon.

I might have borne with this economical diet patiently if I could have got any satisfaction about the great business; but nothing was got ready, nothing begun. At last I saw that I was the victim of the basest imposture; and when I reflected on all the deeds my weakness had allowed to be extorted from me, I realized all the horror of my position.

Forthwith I burst into bitter complaints. Cooper, in a rage, threw away his mask, and might have said—

"C'est à vous de sortir, vous qui parlez en maître;
La maison m'appartient...."

And truly, my own agreement in his hand, he ruled like a despot over the house he had let to me for 25,000 francs; and to make me feel the full weight of his authority, he redoubled his economies, kept under lock and key even the garden seeds which I was no longer allowed to gather for my birds; spoke haughtily to me; poured out abuse on me, and, in a sort of way, kept me under close surveillance.

He had then his mother and sister with him, two veritable furies who joined in all his excesses; and as on every occasion they gave way to their fiery passions, several conflicts took place.

No—I can never understand how my husband could restrain himself under such circumstances!

While I was being thus tormented by my new swindler, Alquier-Caze did not lose sight of me, and still speculating brilliantly on my easy credulity, he endeavoured to approach me once more through this very specious preamble.

"Milady, no doubt you will be astonished at receiving a letter from me; this is what has induced me to write to you.

"This morning a person I do not know, and who would not tell me his name, came to see me. He told me where you are living, and talked a great deal about your case. I cannot and will not trust to paper the communications he made me. They are of importance to you and your position.

"Although I cannot feel much flattered that, being in this country, you have not come to see one who

131

took so much trouble for you, I can never cease to participate in your troubles, and I believe it will be in your interest to tell you what I have learnt.

"I am free only on Sunday. If you think it well for me to come and see you, answer at once, and the day after to-morrow I will be with you.

"Please be prudent and tell no one of my letter, etc."

Curiosity to see him rather than any hope of hearing anything useful decided me to allow him to come. He came, and his constrained manner and ambiguous language soon betraying to me his deceitful plot, I treated him with icy coldness, and made him clearly see that for the future I would have nothing more to do with him. I heard afterwards that his numerous misdeeds had forced him to leave France.

In the meantime I had written to England with orders that the last power of attorney I had so rashly given to the cheat Cooper should not be honoured.

On the first hint of this being learned by my odious agent, he flew into a frightful rage; loaded me with insults, threatened me with his wrath, and put in a distraint on all my effects, to which I responded by a revocation of all the powers I had given him.

We could no longer live with such a scoundrel; so we left Meudon on September 1, 1828, and established ourselves in the Hôtel Britannique.

I need hardly say that on the day we left we had to submit to the grossest of insults in the shape of a ridiculous and minute examination to make sure, as they said, *that we had committed no theft*.

As I pretty often reproached the Baron for having caused

me so many discomforts, I thought I saw that my words had a great effect on him, and his mind seemed much upset. On the fourth day after our change of residence, I saw him go out with a paper in his hand, and asking him when he would be back, he said: "In an hour's time."

While waiting, I went for a walk with my son's former tutor, and on getting back, my first question to the portress was whether my husband had come in.

As she answered in the negative, I ordered dinner to be put off; but the Baron did not return. I began to feel great anxiety, fearing that something had happened to him; but at eight o'clock in the evening I received a packet containing a power of attorney for Ragazzini and a letter for me in these words—

"MY DEAR WIFE,

"I am distressed at having to leave you just now; but business I can't put off longer calls me to Russia. I beg your pardon for not having told you sooner; but I acted in this way so as to avoid the harrowing scenes that would have followed. My agitation is so great that I can say nothing to you but that my conscience does not accuse me of all the wrongs you impute to me. I have told M. Ragazzini to act for you against Driver-Cooper. Some day, I hope, we shall meet again under a more lucky star than the present one. I participate in all your troubles, but I cannot help you. Adieu; *tout à vous*.

"B. DE STERNBERG."

It will well be believed that I cannot describe the grief I felt at finding myself forsaken by him who had so disastrously involved me in so grievous a strife. But his pitiless hand was to strike me a still harder blow.

About the end of the week I received the following letter —

"My dearest Maman,

"My father has just arrived in Geneva, and intends to start for Russia to-morrow with me. I already hear your reproaches; but what can I do?

"Forgive your loving son, and don't think him ungrateful; for I am ready to put my head in the fire if that would be any good to you.

"But what would become of me if I did not obey my father's orders? Don't be afraid; you will always have the whole of my filial love.

"How cruel it is to tear me in this fashion from my darling mother! But what can be done? If you had stayed at Coligny, and if you had listened to my advice, this would not have happened.

"I am hurried. Be comforted; you shall soon have news of me, and believe me always the most loving of your sons.

"Edward Sternberg."

What I felt on reading this was not grief; it was despair. For several days I gave myself up completely to the most acute anguish; at times I wanted to start for Russia; at others I resolved to let myself die.

But at last real maternal love triumphed over affliction, and I realized that it was necessary for the good of my children both to go on living and to remain in France.

Taking fresh courage, I formed the unshakable resolution to suffer and face everything, that I might gain a victory to the advantage and honour of those who were so dear to me in this world.

VIII

Cooper's Rage—Recourse to the Law—First Result of Arbitration—M. Huré—My Letters to Mme. de Genlis—Visit of Saint-Aubin—His Journey—Emissary from Mme. de Genlis—Letters from Saint-Aubin—His Return—Realized Fears—Mr. Mills's Tricks—My Correspondence with the English Ambassador.

While I was lamenting over the unexpected departure of my husband and son, Driver-Cooper, for his part, was loudly complaining, and wanting to force me to go back to his house, which he still kept on calling his *château at Bellevue*, his beautiful *château of Colonnes*.

Maintaining that, as I had been, and was still, his boarder, he said, the usual meals were being served every day for me and my people.

He was eating them by himself—without much trouble, probably!—but still protested, none the less, that I ought to pay him 25,000 francs a year for dinners I refused to eat; and talked a lot of other nonsense.

I wanted to put an end to these impudent molestations, and, as a clause in each of our two famous Ferney agreements submitted any difficulty that might arise to arbitrators, amicably chosen by us, or, in default of that, by the Tribunals of the Seine, I had recourse to the last means.

The arbitrators were appointed, and I explained to them the clever way in which the perfidious Cooper had blinded me, as well as his iniquitous fashion of fulfilling his obligations; I especially brought to their notice that, by the terms of the contract, his lease was to last only for the time taken up by my great affair; and that this had legally come to an end since my revocation of the powers I had given him.

The first decision of the arbitrators, given on September 30, 1828, was in my favour, and annulled the agreement as to the letting of the *manoir* of Bellevue at the rent of 25,000 francs; but, to my great surprise, I found myself sentenced to pay 16,000 of it as a compensation for the time I had spent in that wretched hole and for other expenses I knew nothing about for the most part; an indispensable condition for obtaining the restitution of my effects.

When I had done this, I fixed a day for them to be fetched, and the holder undertook to give them up.

Fresh matter for astonishment.

My servant presents himself and is informed that the removal is opposed at the request of M. Huré, furniture-dealer, in whose favour the honest Cooper had backed my bills.

Luckily for me, the President suspected some intrigue and ordered a severe examination of the books and registers of the opposer, who, less disreputable than his corrupter and not daring to play his part to the end, frankly owned to his odious rôle of catspaw.

The Court, having condemned him in costs, sent back my claim for the return of my bills for the judgment of the same arbitrators who were to pronounce as to the validity of the agreement in virtue of which I had consented to them. But I had to endure such delays that my poor belongings were not returned to me till after six months of waiting,[11] and my old villain raised so many quibbles and difficulties that the discussions relating to the second arbitration lasted a year.

From the very beginning of all these disputes I had been advised to write to the celebrated Comtesse de Genlis, formerly *governess* to the Orleans children,[12] in order to induce her to reveal to me the secrets of this horrible drama, which perhaps she herself had managed.[13]

In consequence, I composed a letter well suited to *her profound modesty and her noble disinterestedness.*

Some days passed and no answer came; and, beginning to think that my letter had not been given to her, I decided to write another, which I sent by sure hands to our chaste Susannah.

MME. DE GENLIS

The next day but one, M. de Saint-Aubin was announced, and there entered a rather good-looking young man, refined and open in manner, who told me he had seen what I had written to Mme. de Genlis, with whom he lived and in whose confidence he was; adding that if I would give him mine, by degrees he would persuade her to speak out.

"Has she not already confessed to me," he went on, "that

your affairs formerly caused her much trouble, and that the evil genius who had bewitched the late Duc de Chartres was an Italian and still living? Anyhow, madame, the only motive I had for coming to see you was the desire to be of use to one who is oppressed."

He then showed me several letters from our *virtuous heroine*, in which she lauded his talents, told him of her own doings, called him her best friend, etc., etc.

In a word, the young rascal left no stone unturned to delude me; and when he thought I was well prepared, he offered to go a journey which, to judge by his hints and mysterious speeches, ought to be to my immense advantage.

Dazzled by this display of verbosity and his gorgeous promises, I sanctioned his plan, and offered him 1000 francs to carry it out. He asked me for 3000, and we split the difference.

In acknowledgment of the sum I handed over to him, all he gave me was this meaningless memorandum: "I have received from Madame la Comtesse de Newborough 2000 francs, on an agreement between us. Given in Paris, December 6th, 1828. S. D. de Saint-Aubin."

A few days later he announced to me his arrival at Nancy, and said he had already got important information.

I had just received this news, when an ill-dressed man holding a paper made his appearance, calling out to me: "Didn't you write this letter to the Comtesse de Genlis?" And as I took it from his dirty and disgusting hands, to see if it was really mine, he went on: "The Comtesse won't have anything to do with your affair, which can't be anything but an imposture. What! you claim to be the daughter of the Duc d'Orléans? For shame! you deserve to be finely laughed at."

I had him turned out at once, throwing my letter, which he wanted to get back, into the fire; and not only this, but I begged a lady, a friend of mine, to call for me upon my considerate confidante to express to her my displeasure and to ask her for the papers I had been foolish enough to send her.

My friend insisted on seeing her, and, after a long delay, she grew angry in her turn, promised haughtily to return everything to me, shut her door and disappeared.

Although my packet never arrived, I thought it would henceforth be beneath me to have any intercourse with such a person, who, doubtless, would have preferred remitting it to her dear adopted son, in the hope of reaping golden harvest from this fresh proof of her boundless devotion.

Meantime, the cunning Saint-Aubin wrote again, assuring me that he was greatly pleased with his mission, and had found out many things, about which he would tell me on his return.

Shortly after he wrote that he had just discovered the dwelling of a very aged Italian woman, the former nurse of Chiappini's son, who possessed a very precious medallion and alone could give me more valuable information than any I had yet got. He promised to bring her to Paris, provided I could enable him to give her a gratuity. To my shame I confess that again I was so foolishly simple as to send him 500 francs, begging him to manage to let me make her acquaintance as soon as possible.

Seven long weeks having passed with no word from him, I began to get impatient, when he took it into his head to send me the well-worn excuse of an unforeseen accident. This is his amusing note—

"Madam, I may truly say that I have come back

from the other world. Some days after receiving your second letter—that is to say, in January last—I had set out for a place I wanted to find. I had hired a carriage for the journey. As the roads were very difficult on account of the ice and snow, the carriage was upset; it was a terrible disaster; I was carried away unconscious, and it was only after six weeks that I began to recover. During the lucid moments of my illness I wished very much to write to you, but I dared not confide in any one.

"For the last fortnight I have been much better. As this misfortune happened to me near Strasburg, I write to you from that town.

"My friends and relations must be very anxious about me, for I have not been able to write to them; besides, it would have alarmed them too much if they had known of my condition.

"I shall be in Paris in eight days.

"I am longing to see you and to relieve the terrible anxiety you must have been in at the total want of news.

"I have done all I could, and have much to tell you.

"Your humble and devoted servant,

"SAINT-AUBIN."

It may well be supposed that I was somewhat surprised that severe suffering should have made him completely forget both the old nurse and the interesting medallion.

Alas! my doubts turned to cruel certainties when I saw him come in plump and blooming, and with a look of long-standing health.

After having at great length bewailed his *unlucky adventure,* he rose, took leave, and contented himself with saying, as he left the room, that he would come again and give me a full report.

Tired of waiting, after a few days I sent to the address he had given me, only to be told that he was known there only as being sometimes seen in the company of other young scapegraces who had left without paying, and that Saint-Aubin was no better than his companions.

This was the end of the adventure.

I have since discovered that this *chevalier d'industrie* was the near relative of the *venerable* Comtesse de Genlis, *née* Ducrest de Saint-Aubin!

While all this was going on, I had need of an English lawyer to manage my London affairs.

A Mr. Mills was recommended to me as a model of integrity. I sent for him; he came, showed me the greatest respect, condoled with me on my troubles; took the liveliest interest in my concerns, and undertook not only to manage everything in England, but to obtain for me, free of interest, the sum necessary to meet the unjust claims of Cooper in Paris.

Delighted to have made his acquaintance, I put myself into his hands; and in a little while he became my guide, my steward, my banker, and my manager.

By his advice, and against my own judgment, I wrote to the British Ambassador to ask his protection against my unworthy extortioner.

To this request his lordship *condescended* to have an answer sent to me in these terms—

"Lord Stuart de Rothesay presents his compliments

to Lady Newborough-Sternberg, and begs her to send him a detailed account of the business. Without this it will not be in his power to be of any service to her.

"The English Embassy, April 22, 1829."

At once I put together my papers and sent them, with the following letter—

"Lady Newborough-Sternberg presents her compliments to Lord Stuart de Rothesay, and, in accordance with the wish expressed in his kind note, sends him the details of her case, begging him to be good enough to give it his consideration.

"If his Excellency should desire fuller information, Lady N.-S. will ask Mr. Mills to give it to him, etc."

Unluckily, amongst my papers there was a mention of my most important affair.

The Ambassador, confounding the two, and fearing to compromise himself, sent the whole back to me with this laconic note—

"Milady, in returning the documents sent to me in your letter of yesterday, I beg you to accept the regret I feel that I cannot give you the help you ask by interfering in a dispute between you and his Most Christian Majesty.

"I have the honour to be your Excellency's most obedient servant,

"STUART DE ROTHESAY."

Astounded at so prompt a change, I seized my pen and wrote—

143

"It appears, Milord, that you have misunderstood my meaning. Please feel quite assured that I asked your help only in my dispute with Cooper. If I had supposed for one moment that you were to be helpful to me in my delicate affair, I should have well deserved the mortification of being refused.

"But I thought I ought to have recourse to you to obtain justice in a scandalous dispute arisen between two subjects of the monarch whose representative you are.

"Is it possible, Milord, that you should regard my complaints with indifference, and that you should refuse me the help you so generously bestow on all those who implore it?..."

Thus ended my correspondence with the noble gentleman, and I refrain from saying anything about his subsequent behaviour.

IX

Ragazzini sent off—Proposal of Mr. Mills—Offers to Cooper—His Account—His Disgust—His Calumnies—My Vindication—Decision of the Arbitrators—Fresh Quibbles—Divers Sentences.

To all my outside troubles were added a host of domestic misfortunes, for the most part caused by the unworthy confidant to whom my husband had, so to speak, handed me over. I mean M. Ragazzini, who, proud of the authority the Baron had conferred on him, became day by day more arrogant, and now took no trouble to conceal his hateful

144

vices.

No longer able to endure his presence, I made up my mind to dismiss him ignominiously.

Being now alone and needing some diversion, Mr. Mills offered me one of his sisters-in-law, whom he described as a real *miracle* of nature. I thanked him for his kindness, but gave an equivocal answer. He returned to the charge, but I still made only complimentary rejoinders.

At last he spoke with such warmth, whether of the dangers of my solitary state, or of the rare qualifications of the young person, that I consented to take her as my *dame de compagnie*.

She came, and I very soon found her to be an insipid creature, to say the least of it, whose wardrobe stood in much more need of my help than I did of her society. The tradesmen's invoices can bear witness to the zeal I displayed on her behalf as well as on that of her sisters and brother-in-law. But what would I not have done for a family whom I considered as my only resource for getting out of the hands of the infamous Cooper?

When the second arbitration concerning the agreement as to the management of the larger affairs took place, I asked for the cancelling of that agreement, offering to make good Cooper's disbursements and fees, deducting only the bills handed over by me on April 1, 1828.

At the invitation of the arbitrators he produced his account, in which a sum of 6,526 francs was placed to my credit.

My counsel, astonished at this, since he had reclaimed only the bills of £75 sterling each, asked for explanations, and it turned out that besides those two bills, Cooper had received another for 5000 francs which, among the many deeds and bills of exchange he had successively extorted from me, I had forgotten. In consequence, I amended my plea, and asked for the deduction of this new amount.

It would be impossible to imagine the disgust of our *honest man* when he realized that he might have hidden for all eternity the existence and the payment of my bill. According to him it was not just that a fit of absence of mind should make him lose £200 sterling.

Unluckily he could not do away with what was written in his account by his own hand; but to evade the consequences of his *fatal* admission he had recourse to calumny.

According to him, every one in Geneva had been alarmed at the first hint of my approaching departure, my debts were so numerous, and my reputation for laxity so well known! Upholsterers and tradesmen had come in crowds, and I had all at once found myself in the toils of Rabelais' terrible quarter of an hour.

Having nothing with which to pay off my debts, I had vainly implored the help of M. Hentsch, a banker of Geneva; but he himself, *poor Cooper*, touched with compassion, had at once handed over to me 5000 francs which he had in his purse, etc.[14]

I should disgust my readers too greatly if I repeated here the vile abuse with which he spiced this heap of inventions.

Anxious to undeceive a public that did not know me, I wrote to Geneva, and found no difficulty in obtaining a large number of excellent testimonials, of which I will quote but three.

1st. "Milady, we have received the letter your ladyship was kind enough to write to us, and have been much grieved at the lies which wickedness and calumny have dared to invent about you; only a consummate scoundrel could be capable of it.

"Messrs. Hentsch have told me that they will write to you at once, so as to undeceive the small number of persons who could have believed this tissue of falsehoods. The Cramers will do the same; and I can assure your ladyship that every one in Geneva who had the pleasure of your acquaintance is indignant at what you must have gone through.

"But we trust the culprit will speedily be punished, and that we shall soon have the pleasure of having you amongst us again, which we look forward to greatly.

"Madame Galiffe asks me to give you her respects, and to assure you of the sincere pleasure it will be to see you again.

"Accept the assurance of my profound respect, and of the great esteem with which I have the honour to be your ladyship's very humble and obedient servant.

"GALIFFE,

"Colonel."

2nd. "Madame, I was less surprised than deeply grieved at the contents of your letter to Colonel Galiffe; for my wife and I felt only too much anxiety as to the result of your journey. M. Cooper has quite justified the opinion of him we formed when we saw him at your house, for we feared just what has happened.

"Good God! into what hands you have fallen! And how could so fine and spotless a character as yours be blackened by calumny?

"But I have no doubt that you have speedily turned aside the shafts of malice. As to what is said about your debts, I can certify that I have known you to be most scrupulous in paying all your accounts; that I have never heard of your being in arrears with any creditor, and that I am in a good position to judge, having had several conversations about your concerns with M. Hentsch, who, I have no doubt, will testify to the same.

"But what need is there, madame, to continue in this strain, or to undertake to clear so unjustly attacked a reputation?

"Many other better-known persons than I will come to your aid, and in a little while you will receive from all sides documents wherewith to crush your vile calumniators.

"I will conclude, madame, by sending you my most sincere wishes that your enemies may get what they deserve, and may their punishment be as certain as all I have said is true.

"My wife asks me to give you all kind messages, and I beg you, Madame la Baronne, to accept the expression of my respect and my sincere attachment.

"J. L. Cramer,

"Lt.-Colonel."

3rd. "Madame, and respected friend; what! there are villains in the world who, not content with having taken advantage of your ignorance of business, venture to attack the reputation of one whose private life it seems to us ought to have been more than safe from the tongue of calumny.

"We are shocked at it, and ready to send you voluminous testimonials as to the high reputation you left behind you here.

"If necessary, we will state in Court that we know you to have been held in constant affection and respect by all around you; that benevolence was your especial virtue, and that your steps were followed by actions recorded in the book of heaven, when unnoticed or unfelt by men.

"We can say that you gave happiness to many here; we can say (though it is impossible that such a question should be put to us), we can say that it is false, absolutely false, that you left debts behind, and that, on the contrary, before you left, you had the forethought to leave 2000 francs on deposit to pay the rent of your country house in case of its not being sub-let; which event happened.

"We can say that your charming son gave the highest hopes of inheriting the striking virtues that distinguish you, and which he could have gained only in the bosom of a mother worthy of all honour and best formed for an example of all that society loves and welcomes.

149

"Speak, Madame la Baronne, only speak! What can we do to communicate to your judges the feelings of the highest esteem which we have for you?

"Your very humble servant,

"H. Hentsch, fils."

It needed nothing more to obliterate the disastrous impressions my audacious calumniator's lies might have made.

I was summoned to declare if I had, or had not, received from him the amount of my bill; and on my formal answer in the negative, the arbitrators of course said to us—

"Since you disagree as to facts, we cannot pronounce for one or the other; we must give our decision according to the wording of the bill. If it was endorsed, 'Sum received in cash,' Mr. Cooper is right; if not, he is wrong. Therefore, produce this bill."

I wrote at once to my London banker to get an authentic copy; but before it arrived, the extension of time for the arbitration expired, and the arbitrators gave their decision. They cancelled the agreement concerning the larger interests, fixed Mr. Cooper's disbursements at 4,169 francs 51; assigned him 3000 francs for his trouble,[15] and ended by making this order—

"We declare and decree that on Mr. Cooper returning the deeds, papers and all other effects, the Lady de Sternberg shall be under the obligation to pay him the sum of 7,169 francs 51; that Mr. Cooper, on payment of the said sum, shall return to her the two bills of £75 sterling each, unless their worth is deducted from the 7,169 francs 51.

"We reserve to both parties their respective rights as to the deduction, claimed by the Lady de Sternberg, of £200 sterling, the amount of the third bill received by Mr. Cooper.

"On the fulfilment by Lady de Sternberg of the above directions, we declare that she shall be freed from all obligations to Mr. Cooper arising out of the agreement of April 27, 1828."

The execution of this judgment could present no difficulties except for that concerning the bill for £200 sterling, with which it could not deal.

A few days later the bill arrived; it was endorsed: "Sum received on my account from the testamentary executors of the late Lord Newborough"; and Cooper had sworn that it was endorsed, "Sum received in cash."

The 5000 francs therefore ought to be deducted from the 7,169 francs 51. Cooper refused to deduct them; I proposed to him to submit this difficulty anew to the arbitrators, who, knowing the business in all its details, could decide on it at once.

An honest man would have gladly accepted this expeditious settlement; but our scoundrel, who had already seen his way to take advantage of his position, absolutely refused.

Having extra-judicially called upon him to name his arbitrator, and on his failing to respond to this summons, I applied to the President of the Court, who assigned me one.

On the day appointed for the meeting of the "friendly arbitrators," Driver-Cooper sent word to them that he opposed their proceeding until after the cancelling of the bills; and they thought themselves bound to abstain from a decision until there had been legal enactment on this opposition.

At the same time my rascal sent me orders to pay him the full sum of 7,169 francs 51, which he must receive at once, so depriving me by his frivolous objections of the power of previously effecting the deduction of the 5000 francs, which had nevertheless been so expressly reserved for me by the decree of the arbitrators. But I knew my man too well not to foresee that after obtaining the payment he demanded, he would take every means to refuse my demand, even to the declinatory plea of the French Courts.

In consequence I made him an actual offer of the sum of 2,169 francs 51, and as to the 5000 francs representing the value of my bill of £200 sterling, I proposed to deposit it in the *Caisse de Consignations*, not to be withdrawn by Mr. Cooper until it was decided that the aforesaid deduction could not be made.

Moreover, I summoned Mr. Cooper to make a declaration of my available effects, and to be ordered to return to me all my deeds, under pain of damages to the amount of 100 francs for each day's delay.

Even this did not stop him, and I was obliged to make an application to the President to make him cease his persecution.

The President having made an order entirely agreeing with my wishes, Cooper appeared disconcerted, and did not dare to appeal against it.

It was in this condition that the case was brought into Court. There my rascal once more took up his rôle, and, as usual, bristled with objections and quibbles which prolonged the disgusting dispute till October 8. All his cunning and ingenuity could not save him from the condemnation he deserved.

But, alas! my triumphs were but funeral honours, and my gains nothing but actual losses.

Yes, my over-great belief in so unworthy a man had cost

me more than 28,000 francs, my peace of mind, and my health.

X

When I found that my troublesome dispute was coming to an end and that I was about to recover both my documents and my own full liberty, I had the following article inserted in several newspapers—

"In the year 1773, two illustrious French personages were travelling *incognito* in Italy, under the names of the Comte and Comtesse de Joinville. On the 16th of April of that same year the Comtesse gave birth to a daughter in the little town of Modigliana. The parents, urged by ambition, resolved to exchange their daughter for the son of a jailer, named Chiappini, whose wife at the same time gave birth to a boy, who has in consequence enjoyed the rank and fortune belonging to the other child. It has pleased Providence to allow this unjust usurpation to last for many years. But, to prove that justice, though sometimes slow, is always sure, it has lately permitted this unnatural action to be brought to light; the proofs were sufficient to convince any impartial mind, and a decisive decree of the Ecclesiastical Court of Faenza, given upon the most undoubted evidence, has pronounced as to the truth of the facts.

"The father, many years ago, met with a violent death; the mother survived him, but has now been eight years dead; and there is no doubt that the parents during their lifetime entrusted certain papers and documents to persons who were then in their confidence.

"It is needless to add that these documents are of the highest importance to the daughter who was deprived of her proper position. In the name of justice and humanity, she entreats any persons who may be in possession of documents concerning this matter, to send such information, in writing, to the Baronne de S., 18 Rue Vivienne, Paris.

"They may feel assured of a large reward from the person concerned."

A few days later I had almost the same words again put in; at last, M. Mills having called a third time at the office of the *Quotidienne*, M. Laurentie said he would like to see me before the third insertion was made, alleging that he could be of much more use to me when he was perfectly acquainted with my affair.

I was urged to receive him, and I fixed a day for his coming.

The first thing he did on seeing me was to give a start of astonishment.

He told me that he had known at once that my paragraph related to the Duke of Orleans, and that, fearing his Highness's anger, he wanted to see my papers before going further.

I at once got together some imperfect copies that had chanced to escape the insatiable Cooper's greedy rapacity, and handed him the parcel.

He strongly advised me against any mysterious or partial publication of my story, but to bring it to the full light of day.

I told him that such was my intention.

"You will do well," he said; "and I assure you your likeness to Louis XIV is so striking that only to see you is to be convinced."

It would not be easy to describe my surprise when, three days later, I received my packet, accompanied, for all apology, by the following brief communication —

"MADAME LA BARONNE,

"I have the honour of returning you the papers you committed to my care.

"I have had an opportunity of tracing the truth to its source, and have ascertained that M. le Duc and Mme. la Duchesse d'Orléans did not quit Paris or the Court in the year 1773."[16]

"Therefore I cannot permit the *Quotidienne* to print a single line concerning the extraordinary and mysterious event spoken of in these papers.

"I have the honour to be, Madame la Baronne,

"Your very humble and obedient servant,

"LAURENTIE."

To astonishment succeeded just indignation when in the numbers for the 2nd and 3rd of November I read what follows—

"The public may have remarked, some time ago, a notice in the *Quotidienne* in which there was mention of a Comte and Comtesse de Joinville, who, in 1773, when in Italy, had a child of the female sex for which a male child was substituted, and information was asked as to this mysterious substitution.

"Whatever may have been the purpose of the person who sent us this notice, it is our duty to declare that we take no responsibility for it.

"We have even been able to ascertain that its publication masks an intrigue in which we could not be expected to meddle, and we retract the notice sent to our office, and which, at first sight, might seem to be simply an announcement relating to family matters."

At first I wanted to force the audacious editor to insert in his journal an answer which would have let every one know of his criminal abuse of confidence, and ask him how he dared brand with the odious name of *intrigue* a claim which, from my papers so trustfully given over to him, he knew to be based on the depositions of numerous witnesses, and on an episcopal judgment given with the most imposing formalities.

But on consideration I decided that my complete Memoirs being about to appear, France and the whole of Europe would do me enough justice after reading them.

I wanted some one to correct the many mistakes which my pen, so unskilled in the French language, had made without taking from my story its original simplicity.

M. Lafont d'Aussonne, author of the *Mémoires universels de la Reine de France,* called on me, discoursed on his literary talents, offered me his services, and succeeded in getting me to give him a copy of my notes. Here is his letter of the next day —

"Madame,

"I have spent part of the night in reading your papers. I find them convincing, and am astonished only at one thing—that you have been so long in attacking the unlawful possessor. I shall have the honour of seeing you this evening at the same hour as yesterday.

"Your very respectful and devoted servant,

"Lafont d'Aussonne."

I was much pleased with his way of looking at it, and with all the arguments with which he supported my interesting affair; but with a swift change of front he wrote to me a few days later—

"However long the time I have devoted to the papers you committed to me, madame, I grudge neither the time nor the work if I may keep your confidence and your esteem. From things I know of and approaching events, I am convinced that your cause has its dangers, and that you must be prepared for oppositions, humiliations, delays and troubles innumerable.

"Your last years will be years of grief and affliction; I am not exaggerating.

"An opportunity is now offered me of rendering you the greatest of services by giving you rest and peace of mind.

"You are a good wife and tender mother; you might, at the same time, give delight to your family and to the excellent persons who have given such proof of their constancy and their devotion by

157

combining with you.

"As for myself, madame, I have no thought but to repeat the assurance of my respectful and sincere devotion.

"LAFONT D'AUSSONNE."

At once I saw through the plot, and wishing to find out what offers would be made me, I replied in such a fashion as to let it be believed that I was quite willing to make concessions.

MARIA STELLA, LADY NEWBOROUGH, BARONNE DE STERNBERG

My friend fell into the trap, loudly applauded my quite futile letter and sent me a curious composition, of which M. d'Aussonne declared he had secretly sent a copy to my adversary.

"MONSEIGNEUR,

"As M. de Broval's illness or sufferings may last some long time, I take the respectful liberty of addressing you directly.

"I have not forgotten that, five years ago, your Royal Highness did me the honour to send for me to your gallery that I might give my opinion on some wrongly-named or doubtful portraits, and that you received me with marked affability.

"Something has now happened, monseigneur, which, in a fashion, brings me again to your notice.

"Lady Newborough, Baronne de Sternberg, having read with great interest at Nice, where she was then living, my *Mémoires universels de la Reine de France*, wished to know its author; and this lady, pleased with my eagerness, has entrusted me with the revision of her own Memoirs written entirely in her own hand, that I may put them into shape and give them a literary style.

"Devoted as my whole life has been to the defence of the greatly unfortunate, I did not hesitate to accept this commission; and I think I have made some improvements in a book good society seems to me to be eagerly expecting, here and elsewhere.

"With my mind full of the strange details contained in these Memoirs, I cannot help looking upon the prodigious noise such revelations will make in the world as *a great political event*; and I ask myself if I should not be doing a good action in endeavouring to find some means for bringing about conciliation and peace.

"There is no room for doubt, monseigneur, that milady, by the advice of her lawyers, will find herself obliged to prove, by numberless traits, character and conduct that the inhuman father, by whom she was forsaken, made the criminal exchange for his *own immoral ends*. After this, we shall see this father, already so notorious, handed over to the judgment of all Europe. As to the gist of the principal question, monseigneur, you must already know everything. You know of Lorenzo Chiappini's clear statement, made but a few moments before his death; you know of the numerous depositions of so many candid and unexceptionable witnesses; you know of the solemn decree of the august Tribunal which restored to Maria Stella her original position, and as a consequence, her rights.

"From the moment that striking judgment was pronounced, milady was enabled fearlessly to sign herself *née de Joinville*; and we have no other Joinvilles but the Princes of the House of Orleans.

"The documents obtained in Italy are already very considerable; those discovered in France are not less so; and the two journeys in Italy are proved.

"To these remarkable details I beg your Highness to be pleased to add the following facts.

"Milady's profile is extraordinarily like that of Madame la Dauphine; seen at three-quarters her face is the image of that of Mademoiselle d'Orléans, etc. Lord Newborough, her eldest son, bears so strong a resemblance to Louis XIV, and her second son, M. Chevalier Wins (*sic*) to the late Comte de Beaujolais, that the artists are amazed.

"And now, monseigneur, I will add, by your gracious permission, a fact which is as extraordinary and seems miraculous; the two brothers Chiappini, each the image of his father, have the honour of resembling you. The inhabitants of Florence and Modigliana are all agreed on this point.

"I have given you but a short summary of this important affair, known to no one better than to myself since I have had everything under my own eyes.

"My great respect for the name of Bourbon leads me to hope that confidential matter of this kind may not be told in the market-place, to become the fable or the romance of all parties. With all my heart I desire that the life of our beloved Duc de Bordeaux may be spared; but if, by a stroke of fate, that fragile olive-branch were snatched from France, the Salic Law would call your children to the throne, and it might be painful, perhaps dangerous, for them not to have public opinion with them.

"You anticipate, monseigneur, what would be my respectful advice, and I beg you to see in my action no motives but those dictated by kindness, wisdom and prudence.

"The excellent milady, who admires my works, has favoured their author with her partial confidence; but I have the honour of writing to you without her knowledge.

"I wish to help her to the ease of mind so astounding a trial could not fail to destroy; and, if you have sufficient trust in me to accept me as intermediary, I feel a secret presentiment that I shall be able to induce her to make peace.

"I am a daily witness of her respect and admiration for Louis XIV, Henri IV, etc., whom she looks upon as her ancestors; but I know, too, that she adores her beloved Edward, her youngest son, from whom she has been cruelly separated; and by this very natural way I think I may reach her heart.

"If so, I shall rejoice at having restored her to life and peace, and to have spared you, monseigneur, an unpleasant dispute through which your children, sooner or later, must have suffered.

"Allow me with the greatest respect to sign myself your Royal Highness's very humble and obedient servant,

"LAFONT D'AUSSONNE."

All this inspired me with invincible dread of a man who, like so many others, thus played me false. To escape his snares I began by politely refusing to see him; then, under various pretexts, I asked him to send back my books and papers, and tried to make him understand my very natural apprehensions. His letters will prove the accuracy of my statements—

1st. "Madame, I have the honour to return you the books relating to the great affair. I will also collect the papers you ask for and this evening you shall receive them in a sealed parcel. I like to take back such important things myself.

"For God's sake don't allow yourself to have any doubt of me or my doings. I am doing what is for the best, and for your sole and veritable benefit.

"If I asked to see you for a moment, it was to tell you of a most important matter which has to do with what you were told in Italy—that a *French ecclesiastic knew a great secret concerning all this.*

"While I write to you, a person in my confidence is

taking the necessary steps for discovering what the Duke wishes to do as to the matter about which I wrote to him.

"Rest assured, milady, that God decreed your acquaintance with me, and that you will never find another with a heart so good and large as mine, or so noble a probity.

"But your misfortunes have naturally made you timid and suspicious, and you may feel quite certain that I am too reasonable to take offence. Your most respectful and devoted servant," etc.

2nd.—"Madame, What I told you in my letter of yesterday rests on the evidence of two persons, of whom one, aged and infirm, and of a timid and nervous disposition, has told me what she knows, and by her explanations has enabled me to explain to myself things which formerly did not sufficiently influence me, for I was the best friend and vindicator of *him who knew all.*

"The other person, who is still alive, will play no part whatever in all this, so greatly does she dread the vengeance of the Duke of Orleans.

"But I, who do not fear him, promise you that, if *we go on acting in unison,* I will state and proclaim everything.

"How could you, madame, suppose for one moment that my actions concealed any plot—actions as clear as day?

"After making a thorough examination of your case, I perceived many probabilities, but, unfortunately, not enough proofs; and that is why, as an honourable and kindly man, I advised you to consent to a compromise, supposing your wealthy adversary able to make up his mind to a sacrifice.

"In this way you would have gained an increase of fortune to the benefit of your son, while the Prince, *real* or *supposed*, would have retained the votes and the respect of the common people which your Memoirs and the noise of the trial must inevitably have lost for him.

"No, milady, Mme. Fleury and I have not joined in any plot against you; since that wicked Irishwoman wanted the Duke to crush you by his power without giving you anything out of his riches; while what I desire is that if he and you come to some arrangement, he shall make over to you a considerable sum.

"The letter I sent him is surely proof enough of that.

"Is that letter, wherein I made such outspoken and humiliating statements, nothing in your eyes? Is that possible? And what can I do, Madame, to prove to you my sincerity and integrity?

"Oh! what a lesson for me!

"I must end here a letter I did not think to make so long.

"I have served you zealously, milady; and I don't regret it, for I believe your cause to be a just one in the sight of God and of nature.

"I withdraw without resentment, although I am much hurt by the insult offered to me.

"If the Duke comes to know what has taken place, he will be much rejoiced, for he dreads my pen and the strength of my writings.

"With all respect, madame," etc.

In spite of all these protestations, he could not win back my confidence, and I would have nothing more to do with him.

Mills's sister-in-law was still with me; but for the last few days I had noticed a complete change in her for which I could not account and which she would explain to me only by pleading indisposition.

One morning her younger sister made her appearance and told me she wished to take her sister back with her to stay while the carnival lasted, as while she was with me she had no chance of enjoying the entertainments connected with it.

Glad of this opportunity, I replied at once—

"With pleasure; I should be very sorry to put her out. Let her stay at home as long as she likes."

The two ungrateful creatures went off at once to collect the munificent gifts I had made them, packed up their parcels, and, from that moment, never once took the trouble to inquire after me.

I saw at last—but too late—what sort of family this was, and to what a set of people I had so generously given myself over.

It was only with the greatest difficulty that I managed to get a statement of my accounts, and when I did receive it, I found myself finely tricked!

For a few private consultations of no importance, and a few drives about Paris, the considerate lawyer was content with asking me the *bagatelle* of 6000 francs; *inadvertently* indebted me with £300 sterling, and exacted the rigorous payment to him of interest for which he had promised I should not be liable!

I held my tongue, hoping he would not force me to divulge what I knew of myself or had heard spoken of.

My eldest son had known him better than I did; he wrote later to me from Marseilles that he had always had strong suspicions about him and had never ceased to look upon him as a professional humbug.

This letter from the young Lord Newborough, as well as showing the great affection he had for me, gave me besides two strong grounds for consolation in the midst of my trouble, by assuring me of the restoration of his own health and of his undying attachment to my dear Edward.... I knew that for some time he had been suffering from a weak lung, and remembering his antecedents, I had felt grave fears; on the other hand, the future of my third son was a source of painful anxiety to me.

But his kind brother did away with all my troubles on both matters by telling me that the mild climate of southern Europe had quite restored his strength, and by asking me to tell Edward that he could henceforth look upon Glynllifon Castle as his own house.

Could anything be sweeter to the heart of a loving mother? And it was not the only sign of filial love that came to ease my mind. The youngest of my children never failed from time to time to send me the expression of his ardent love for me. This is one of his recent letters —

"I am delighted to see that our *great affair* is beginning to get cleared up and looks so well. I wish with all my heart that it may go in our favour, and that you may at last be able to enjoy some compensation for the vicissitudes and cares and worries which you have had to bear for the last seven or eight years.

"Believe me, my dear mother, my most earnest prayer is that I may see you win the victory in a trial you have so much at heart and which so nearly concerns our family and your name, etc."

XI

The Cause of my Delay—My Trustfulness—Louis-Philippe, Duke of Orleans—Louis-Philippe-Joseph, his Son—Chief Vices of the Last —Bad Son—Bad Husband—Bad Father Bad Friend—Bad Citizen— Consequent Results.

I ask my readers to forgive me for having so long entertained them with so many tiresome details. I had no thought at first of doing so, but the recent attempts at the most impudent frauds[17] have more and more fully convinced me that I cannot make too well known the various events which have brought about the deferring of my just claims.

And if my silence since I succeeded in getting back my deeds from the hateful Cooper causes some surprise, it must be told that they were hardly once more in my possession before I handed them over to a lawyer of reputation, who, after keeping them a couple of months, wrote to me that, before definitely undertaking my case, he wished, through the medium of M. de Broval or M. Dupin,[18] to get leave to make researches in the archives of the house of Orleans.

"The result of this step," he said, "would be decisive, and, when it had been taken, we could decide as to the following up or the relinquishing of the trial."

It will be believed that I could not consent to be thus put at the mercy of my adversary. I asked for the return of my papers; but once more I could not get them without the payment of 100 francs for the time my *comic* lawyer had thought good to make me lose.

I then decided to have recourse to one of those *colossal celebrities* whose sublime eminence seems to place them so high above the fatal bait of bribes;[19] and these were at first his fine promises—

"Madame la Baronne, I have not yet been able to examine the papers you were kind enough to send me. I propose to devote the whole day to them to-morrow, and I will at once give you my opinion on this *important* business.

"Pray accept, madame, the humble respects of your obedient servant,

"B. F."

Who could believe that more than fifty days after I received this letter, my packet had not even been opened, and that the *important* business rested in oblivion?

At last I put it into the hands of a man whose excellent references proved him worthy of my confidence; he will not abuse it, and most certainly neither he nor those he will employ in my service will behave like those who, acting for me in the Cooper business, so cruelly ground me down.

Yes, I hope Providence has not quite forsaken me, and that the day of victory will come; the many valuable discoveries the base machinations of my enemies have been unable to prevent me making, vouch for it, and give me confidence amidst my many tribulations. Kindly lend me your ears still.

In 1773, at the time of the infamous substitution, these

were the members of the house of Orleans.

The Prince of that name was Louis-Philippe, who married first Louise-Henriette de Bourbon-Conti, and, secondly, Madame de Montesson; but this last union was always kept secret.

Of the first marriage was born Louis-Philippe-Joseph, then commonly called Duc de Chartres, who, in his turn, became Duke of Orleans, a title he gave up later to assume the ludicrous nickname of Egalité, under which he made himself so ignominiously notorious. He had married Mademoiselle Louise Marie Adélaïde, daughter of the Duc de Bourbon Penthièvre, who died in 1821, under the name of the Dowager Duchess of Orleans.

Louis-Philippe-Joseph is precisely the person who, according to a host of admitted facts, *seems* to us to have been the guilty perpetrator of the criminal exchange; I say *seems*, for submitting beforehand to the final decision of my judges, I will do nothing to prejudice it.

I will not say, with the historians of his life,[20] that the Duc de Chartres, when scarcely out of his boyhood, showed the most depraved tastes, and took no pleasure but in wickedness.

I will not say that from his youth upwards his degrading vices made him the object of universal contempt, and ended by earning for him the vilest names.

I will not repeat that in his inextinguishable passion for riches he was not afraid to show the greatest impatience at the prolongation of his father's life; that, not satisfied with degrading himself, he was willing publicly to dishonour her who had borne him in her bosom, and shamelessly forswore his glorious descent from the most august blood.

I will not repeat that his wife had the constant affliction of finding her efforts to lead him into the ways of a wise moderation quite useless, and that she had to endure hardships of all sorts from a husband both hard and unfaithful.

I will not repeat that he pitilessly sent the sad fruits of his profligacy to the asylum for the poor, and that his legitimate children, given over very early into the hands of strangers, were never the objects of his care, seldom of his endearments.

THE DUCHESS OF ORLEANS

LOUISE MARIE ADÉLAÏDE DE BOURBON-PENTHIÈVRE
WIFE OF PHILIPPE-ÉGALITÉ

I will not repeat that, bad son, bad husband, bad father, he could not fail to be a bad friend, and that many of his confidants were the victims of his perfidy or his rage.[21]

I will not repeat that his presumptuous rebellion, his implacable hatred for the best of kings; the murderous

172

outcries against him he so shamelessly raised, and which, even in his own eyes, proved him the most hateful of citizens, forced from him that admission, as true as humiliating, "I would as soon be guillotined as banished, for where is the country that would receive me?"

But no more—for I blush as I write these lines and my heart bleeds with shame!

Besides, does it need more to represent the man we have just described as quite capable of the crime we think we have the right to impute to him?

Still, we admit that the reality of a thing cannot be deduced from its mere possibility, so we will enforce it by arguments of quite another nature.

XII

An Incontestable Principle—Title and Fief of Joinville—Travels under that Name—The Comte's Titles—His Description—His Character —Deposition of the Signora Galuppi-Toschi—Certificate of the Conte Falopio—That of the Priest Carlo Brunone—Letter from Baron Vincy—Attestation of M. D.—Summary.

Identity of name, title, description, character, position, time and place, are doubtless enough to establish identity of person, or nothing would be able to prove it.

Let us apply this clear principle to the matter in hand, and it will end in proof.

1st. *The name.* Let us remember that the chief agent of the hateful substitution was a Frenchman called Louis, Comte de Joinville. Now, as history and the whole of the aristocracy are silent on the matter, we cannot even imagine

173

that this title in 1773 belonged to any one not of the Orleans family. Let us see if it could then be found *in* that family.

The Fief of Joinville, raised to a barony at the beginning of the eleventh century, and to a principality under Henri II, after passing successively to several lords, had at last fallen into the female line by the death, on March 16, 1675, of the Duc de Guiche, Prince de Joinville; and *Mademoiselle*, the daughter of Gaston de France, having inherited it in her own right from her maternal grandmother, Catherine-Henriette de Joyeuse, Duchesse de Guise, left it by will to her cousin-german, Philippe de France, *Monsieur*, only brother of Louis XIV, and head of the Orleans branch. Whence it follows that this principality is actually patrimonial in that family, and that the Duc de Chartres, son of its chief, had the right to call himself by that name.

I say more: open the books written about him, and the frontispiece will show that he was not only Duc de Valois, de Nemours, de Montpensier, d'Etampes, but also Comte de Beaujolais, de *Joinville*, de Vermandois, and de Soïssons.[22]

I say still more: that is precisely the name under which he and his wife were accustomed to travel.

In 1778 she assumed it to go to Holland; he had taken it in 1777 to visit the Netherlands; the year before it was the title borne by the Duchess during the whole of her tour in Italy;[23] and to speak only of the year of the exchange, the newspapers of the day forbid any doubt that, under that name, and in the summer, the Duke had made a pretty long journey.[24] And worthy witnesses, whose valuable evidence we shall presently quote, declare that the august couple bore that title precisely at the time of the exchange and in the very districts where this horrible agreement was made.[25]

2nd. *The Rank.* According to the decree of Faenza, the

174

Comte de Joinville was a French nobleman; almost all the witnesses testified to his being rich and powerful, and if we may believe the evidence of one who ought to have known more than any one else, since he had it direct from the man who no doubt had categorically interrogated the Comte after his arrest at Brisighella—he was nothing less than a *prince in disguise.*[26]

It will be remembered, too, that having been led before the Cardinal-Legate at Ravenna, the Cardinal, on recognizing him, welcomed him warmly, affectionately embraced him, and at once set him entirely at liberty.

Now, it must be pointed out that the etiquette of the Roman Church is that Cardinals must embrace only the members of reigning houses, and it could have been only the consideration due to so august a rank that could have cut short the prosecution already set on foot by the inexorable agents of the Inquisition.

Now, supposing the titles of *Comte de Joinville, a great French nobleman belonging in 1773 to a reigning family* to be united in a single person, who would not at once recognize Louis-Philippe-Joseph?

3rd. *The Description.* The Comte de Joinville, the Italian witnesses tell us, had a fine figure; he was rather stout, had a brownish complexion, a red and pimply nose, and splendid legs.

But is not this the exact description of the Duc de Chartres as given me by the Abbé de Saint-Fare, who was his natural brother? A description agreeing completely with that of all who knew him. Here is one among many written by a man who had, so to speak, always lived with him—

"Louis-Philippe-Joseph was a fine man in every sense of the word. His figure, of more than middle height, was gracefully and faultlessly proportioned. The lower part of his body, from the waist downwards, could not have been better made; the rest was rather heavy, but this stoutness was not ungraceful.

"As a result of his debauches, his nose and the lower part of his forehead were covered with small red pimples; and this sort of mask, which in fact disfigured him, but which he owed to his dissolute life and not to nature, made many people say that his face was hideous."[27]

4th. *Character.* The Comte de Joinville's habits led him to extreme familiarity with people of low condition, and to great generosity where the success of his ambitious projects was concerned; the positive evidence of witnesses, his sudden intimacy with the jailer, and the presents he made him, leave no room for doubt on that question. But by these signs how can we do anything but believe in the portrait drawn by all historians alike of the Duc de Chartres?

"He loved," they say, "to mix with the crowd, and was never so happy as when he was able to cast off restraint and etiquette; he had a lively and caustic wit, liked to banter his inferiors, and showed no displeasure at their bantering him. Despite the avarice of which he gave so many proofs, which went so far as to make him say that 'a crown in his pocket was worth more to him than all public esteem,' he made no difficulty in scattering his sordid gains with profusion, either to obtain nominations to the States-General or to gain the affection of the great nation he wished to captivate."[28]

5th. *The Circumstances.* We have seen that the Comte de Joinville had some reason to fear that his wife would never give him a male child, and that, in that case, he was afraid of losing a great inheritance absolutely depending on the birth of a son.

Now all the world knows that, in 1773, the Duchesse de Chartres, though in the full bloom of her radiant youth, had, in the four years of her marriage, borne only one daughter, who died at birth on the 10th of October, 1771.[29]

Her ambitious and covetous husband must therefore have greatly dreaded not only the fading away of his flattering hope of winning for his line the good graces of his compatriots, so as to obtain from them the *happy transference* of that crown of France, the object of so many longings, so many intrigues, so many secret manœuvres—it may be obscure crimes—but also to fail in concentrating on his family the whole affection of his father-in-law, the richest of princes, who, still only forty-eight years old, had, since the death of his wife,[30] pretty often shown his intention of contracting a second alliance.[31]

Here again, one feels, the identity is absolute. Finally, let us come to the point which seems to us to sum up everything, and is the most important and the best proved of all.

6th. *The Time and Place.* It was in the spring of the year 1773 that on the heights of the Apennines and in a diocese under the rule of the Papal States, the Comte de Joinville, by means of a most atrocious agreement, succeeded in securing an heir to his name and his lofty hopes.

Can it be true that Louis-Philippe-Joseph and his wife were actually in those districts at that time?

Let us boldly declare that there is no doubt about it.

During my stay at Genoa I learnt that at Reggio there lived a lady formerly in the service of the d'Este family, and who had heard the mysterious journey spoken of.

It will be easily believed that I lost no time in writing to her, and in her turn she made no delay in answering my questions, and assured me she would willingly testify, in a Court of Law if necessary, to everything she had told me.

Delighted at this promise, I gave my orders so as to make sure of a properly drawn-up document.

I chose my lawyer; a proxy was appointed for the Comte and Comtesse de Joinville and any other person absent interested in the case.

In a word, all preliminary formalities having been duly performed, the interrogation was carried out, *in consideration of her circumstances*, at the lady's own house.

After having sworn to speak the whole truth, and being questioned as to the reason of her appearance, her age, her domicile, and her memory, she answered—

"It is in order to obey the command I have legally received from M. le Président that I have consented to this examination. I am sixty-four years old; I live at Reggio, my native town, and I was actually born in the palace of S. A. S. the Duchess Maria-Teresa Cybo d'Este, where my late father, Josophat Galuppi, held the post of auditor of accounts and wardrobe keeper to the Duke Francesco.

"My memory is very good, and I have a clear recollection of things that happened in my young days."

Asked as to whether, while the aforesaid Duchess was living at Reggio, a certain remarkable prince and princess had come there, she answered—

"During the year 1773, and, it seems to me, in the late spring, their Royal Highnesses the Duc Louis-Philippe de Chartres and his wife, the Duchesse Louise-Marie, passed through this town, on their way, I think, from the Papal States.

"I know this because I was present when Count Manetti,

the Duchess Maria-Teresa Cybo's major-domo, was sent to the hotel to welcome the aforesaid Prince and Princess and invite them to the Court. I know it also because I was in a back room when Count Manetti came back, and I quite distinctly heard him say that their Highnesses sent their thanks, but could not accept the invitation, partly because of the incognito they wanted to preserve, as they were travelling under the name of the *Comtes de Joinville, French,* and partly because of the short time they were staying."

Questioned as to whether she knew of any visit of this Prince and this Princess of Chartres to the town at any other time than the above, she answered—

"In 1776, just at the time of the fair in the month of May and when several other princes were also at Reggio, this same Princesse Louise-Marie de Chartres arrived in this town and stayed here till June. She lived in the Giucciardi Palace which my father had got ready for her by order of the Duke Francesco. This time I saw her come to the Court where I was then living. When she came, every one told me she was the Duchesse de Chartres, and it was as such that she was known and saluted by all persons of distinction."

After these questions the examination was gone over again in the order of the records of the trial which the notary public read to this valuable witness, who said—

On the first: "It is quite true that during the spring of the year 1773 their Serene Highnesses the Duc Louis-Philippe de Chartres and the Duchesse Louise-Marie, his wife, passed through Reggio on their way from the Papal States; and that the same Princess in 1776, with other Princes, came to the fair being held at Reggio in the month of May."

On the second: "It is equally true that the aforesaid Prince and Princess were travelling *incognito* and with a small suite, and called themselves the *Comte and Comtesse de Joinville.*"

179

On the third: "It is also the absolute truth that at the news of their arrival in Reggio, the Duchess Maria-Teresa Cybo d'Este sent her major-domo, Count Manetti, to welcome these illustrious personages and to ask them to come to Court. But they did not accept the invitation, alleging the *strict incognito they were keeping*, and the preparations already made for an early departure. And all this I know for the reasons already given."

Finally, to other minor questions put to her she gave pertinent answers: that she professed the Catholic religion; that she married the noble Signore Maria-Toschi of Reggio; that she was not a relation of mine, nor connected with me in any way; that her statement had not been prompted by any one, and that she had been guided solely by her love of right and justice.

Her deposition having been read, she ratified it and confirmed it by her signature.

In the letter she did me the honour of writing to me she mentions two things omitted in the interrogatory: i.e. *that the answer given to the Count Manetti had often since been repeated to her by the people about the Court, and that the illustrious travellers, after spending the night in the hotel they had come to, left very early the next morning.*

After such satisfactory evidence as this I sought further, and found means for fully corroborating it.

First, this is the declaration of one who occupies a very distinguished position —

"To give homage to truth, I testify to the whole world that towards the spring or the beginning of summer, of either the year 1772 or 1773—I am not sure which, but I am certain that it was either one or the other—his Royal Highness, the Duke of Orleans, passed through Reggio, where he slept one night, and I remember his appearance perfectly. *Of middle height, rather stout; a full face that looked as if it were pitted with the small-pox, pimply; a red nose, and rings in his ears*:

"This highly respectable personage was travelling incognito with a woman who was said to be his wife, and under the name of the Comte *de Joinville*. I can all the better attest and confirm this fact to any one, let him be who he may, because at that time I was at the Court of Modena and in the service of his Serene Highness, Ercole III of glorious memory.

"In testimony whereof I affix to my signature the arms of my family.

"Bᴇʀɴᴀᴅɪɴ Gʀɪʟᴇɴᴢᴏɴᴇ-Fᴀʟᴏᴘɪᴏ,

"Chamberlain to his Imperial Highness,
the Archduke of Austria, etc."

In support of these conclusive declarations there is also the following—

"The undersigned, of the town of Alessandria in Piédmont, where he resides; sixty-seven years of age; formerly professor of rhetoric, pensioned by his Majesty the King of Sardinia after having served forty years; being still quite sound in mind, recollects, as well as if it had taken place yesterday, and is ready to take his oath that it was about fifty years ago, though

181

on account of the lapse of time he cannot absolutely swear to the year, that with his own eyes he saw the Duke of Orleans, who then bore the title of Duc de Chartres, pass through Alessandria, coming from Italy and going towards Piédmont.

"In proof whereof he declares that he saw him in his barouche which, with his large suite, waited more than half-an-hour before the Countess Govone's palace, a short distance from the post-house, for what reason nobody knew.

"The undersigned stopped about the same length of time, and remembers that it was in the morning, but has only a faint recollection of the features of this nobleman. He feels certain it was in the summer, and affirms that this is the exact, unalloyed and whole truth.

"In testimony whereof he will affix his signature to it in order that it may serve as an authentic and historical document.

"Alessandria, December 17, 1824.

"The Priest, CARLO BRUNONE, etc."

M. le Baron de Vincy de la B., in a letter he was so good as to write me lately, declares in set terms that *"being in the bosom of his family in 1773, news was spread about in the country that the Duc de Chartres had passed through Berne under the name of Monsieur le Comte de Joinville."*

Which, according to the reiterated assertions of d'Alquier-Caze,[32] would seem to prove that the Prince crossed Switzerland either in going to Italy or on his return.

And finally, M. D., formerly attached to the Orleans family, testifies that the late *Madame the Dowager-Duchess had*

182

made one journey to beyond the Alps before that of 1776; and though he only dimly remembers that it was in 1773, he knows for certain that the incognito name was that of Comtesse Joinville, etc.

Therefore, to sum up, between Louis-Philippe-Joseph, Duc de Chartres, and Louis, Comte de Joinville, perpetrator of the shameful substitution, there is no difference; everything about them is identical, everything proves, everything shows them to be the same person, one and the same individual.

XIII

Circumstances in my Favour—Incognito of the Princes—The Journey of 1776—Extraordinary Precautions—The Duke's Attention to his Wife—Sudden Alteration—Delivery of the Princess—Complaisant Witnesses—Parliament Absent—Dread of Self-betrayal—Secret Sorrows—Mutual Indifference—Speech of Louis XVI—Others made by d'Orléans—Striking Resemblances—Important Traces.

My task would doubtless be finished if there were no question but of inspiring confidence and giving conviction; but when I think of the advantageous position of him I am going to fight, can I be too anxious to equip myself with weapons and support?

Let us therefore consider certain circumstances which furnish us with further arguments in our favour.

1st.—When, wishing to rid those who will receive him of the strict rules of a tiresome etiquette, a prince resolves to travel under the little-known name of one of his estates, he takes care to make public his voluntary metamorphosis, so that, under the borrowed title, none will fail to recognize him who bears it for the moment; and, far from avoiding the palaces of kings, he visits them in order to enjoy their delights more at his ease.

As an instance, let us take the journey of 1776.

Madame de Chartres, having accompanied her husband to Toulon, where he was to embark for his campaign at sea, resolved to visit the Peninsula, without having previously obtained the permission of the Court.[33]

Surely she ought to have taken every care to conceal this *freak*, for which she expected to be banished at least.[34]

Despite this fear, she had it pompously announced that she should travel under the name of Comtesse de Joinville, published her itinerary, showed herself everywhere in public, and everywhere accepted the homage paid to her.[35]

Why, then, was nothing of all this done three years earlier? Why this profound silence, this impenetrable mystery? Why the *secret incognito*, as the witnesses call it? Why did the Duke and Duchess wish to remain unknown, even to the extent of going to an inn, in a town over which their nearest relations reigned,[36] and preferring to pass the night at a hotel rather than accept the invitation sent them to come to Court?

Do not these precautions, this secrecy, point to the committing of a crime, and a crime still far more heinous than that of disregarding the deference due to one's sovereign?

But let us ask, what was that crime?

Point it out to us!

In Heaven's name, could we be told of any other but that very one with which so many incontestable proofs have made us acquainted?

2nd.—During his wife's first pregnancy, the Duc de Chartres never left her side, redoubled his endearments as her time approached, gave up his former evil courses and behaved to the Princess in the most exemplary manner. "Which," says a writer, "gave immense delight to the Duke of Orleans, and still more to M. le Duc de Penthièvre."[37]

True to this way of behaving, in 1773, he did not leave the Duchess during the months preceding my birth; the most he did was to take a short journey to Chanteloup to see the Duc de Choiseul;[38] while after the month of April it was nothing but a series of absences on his part, excursion upon excursion, journey upon journey;[39] and, so far from exercising any restraint, or restricting himself in any way, he spent the whole day with jugglers and pickpockets, cast about for new ways of sinning, and carried his excesses and debauchery to such a pitch as to amaze and shock the by no means susceptible servants of the Palais Royal.[40]

What are we to conclude from so great and sudden a change?

One of two things: either that the Duchess was no longer *enceinte*, or that the Duke had ceased to care about the child she might give him.

This second hypothesis is evidently inadmissible, especially when we remember that the stillbirth of 1771 must naturally fill his ambitious spirit with the gravest fears.

And if he had become so indifferent to the birth of a firstborn, why, six years later, did he express such delight on finding himself the father of a third son?

We must perforce come back to the first supposition, and acknowledge the delivery of the Princess as already accomplished; which entirely agrees with the account of certain inhabitants of Forges,[41] who state that she left their town towards the end of July 1772, with all the signs of the beginning of a pregnancy which would naturally find its termination in the following April.

But if she was no longer *enceinte* in April 1773, was it not impossible that on the 6th of October of the same year she should have given birth to the *Duc de Valois*?[42]

What is told about the time of that confinement is therefore a fable, and a fable of which my story alone explains the motive.

3rd.—It is evident that this event, which was said to have happened five and a half months after I was exchanged, required no precautions if it was a reality; but, on the other hand, very many if it was a pretence.

Accordingly, it was not in the parish church and in public, nor even in the Palais-Royal Chapel, but in some unascertained spot in that dwelling, that the child, born, it was said, at three o'clock in the morning, was privately baptized in the presence of two obscure witnesses in the service of the Orleans family. No Minister of the King's, no Gentleman of the Court was to be seen; in a word, no one was there of whose devotion there could be any doubt.

And that is not all; in the *Gazette de Modène*, called *Le Messager*, No. 44, Nov. 3, 1773, we read under date of Paris, October 11—

"Every one knows that here, on the birth of sons of the royal blood, a report is drawn up in evidence, in the presence of Parliamentary Commissioners who sign it.

"This formality was neglected in the case of the Duc de Valois, and all that was done was to add to the report made on the occasion the words, *Parliament absent*.

"The report was presented to the King for his signature, and it is said that, paying no attention to these words, his Majesty at once signed it."

But the thing, according to the journal we quote, seemed so astonishing that the public, not understanding it, thought to discover in it a sign foretelling very great political events.

4th.—The journey of 1776 had been long planned, and even before leaving Paris there was a positive intention of carrying it out.[43]

Nevertheless it was only in a letter dated from Antibes that the Duchess told the King of her plan, assuring him there had been no premeditation, and alleging, as excuses, her wish to see her grandfather, the Duke of Modena.[44]

But why was this excellent excuse sent from afar; why not dare to give it in person; why put oneself under the sad necessity of lying about it?

Ah! no doubt one feared for one's own countenance; one feared to blush in speaking the word *travel*, and, above all, the name of Italy; one might dread the withering look of a sovereign to whom indiscreet tongues might already have revealed everything.

5th.—On her return from this same journey, the Princess had hardly crossed the boundary of her own country when, as reported by Mme. de Genlis, *she burst into tears*.[45]

Now, these tears, after a short and voluntary absence, a simple pleasure-trip, would surely have been senseless tears if they were caused by nothing, as pretends our *veracious* historian, but joy at being once more on French soil.

Would it not be more natural, more reasonable, to attribute them to importunate memories, for ever connected with the country just left?

6th.—M. Delille, the Dowager's private secretary, tells us in his journal[46] that this lady *confided to her father-in-law hidden troubles which she dared not reveal to the Duc de Penthièvre for fear of grieving him too greatly.*

Can it be said that this refers to the grief caused to the Duchess by her husband's misconduct?

Alas! there was no secret about that; everything was but too well and publicly known; and it is to be supposed that Madame de Chartres would have preferred going for comfort to her virtuous father to complaining about it to the Duke of Orleans, who, in such matters, was no more blameless than his son.

These hidden troubles, requiring so much discretion, must therefore have been of quite another nature, and arose from a different cause.

7th.—The sensitive Princess could never reconcile herself to seeing her children given over to the management of a *governess*. Her complaints never ceased; over and over again she made warm and urgent protests.[47]

Yet who would believe it? These cares and anxieties had nothing to do with the one of her sons who, by right of primogeniture, would have seemed most likely to be most dear to her.

If he informs her that he will be much away with his friend,[48] *she is quite willing; assures him that what suits him will always suit her, and tells him that she does not want to restrain him in any way.*[49]

Whence arose such indifference in a heart otherwise so warm?

And, on the other side, could real filial love, the love

nature must perforce create, exist in one who thought himself lucky that he was not obliged to go to see his *mother* more than twice a week,[50] and whose affection for his governess was so far greater than that he felt for *his own parents*?[51]

8th.—His reputation having become somewhat inconvenient, Louis-Philippe-Joseph, in 1782, went to Versailles to ask permission from Louis XVI to absent himself.

"The King," writes an historian, "received him rather coldly, and answered him in words to this effect—

"I have a Dauphin; Madame may perhaps be enceinte; Monsieur le Comte d'Artois has several children. You can do as you please. I do not see in what way you can be of use to the country; so go when you like and return when it seems good to you."

Why this momentary silence and thoughtfulness, if it were not to remember a fact about to be the object of veiled rebuke from august lips? And what fact? What cause for so severe a reprimand?

According to all evidence it related to the *paternity* of the traveller, and to the dangers with which his absence might have threatened the succession to the crown if it had not been for the existence of several children of the elder branch.

Who would not feel sure that the monarch, knowing of the whole adventure, took this opportunity of moving the culprit to shame and repentance?

9th.—The Convention, after the defection of Dumouriez, having, at its sitting of the 4th of April, 1793, ordered that the citizens Egalité and Sillery were to be watched, Sillery mounted the tribune and stammered out these words: "If my son-in-law is guilty, he ought to be punished; *I remember Brutus* and his sentence on his own son, and I will imitate him."

Then came Orleans, and, as he gazed at the bust of the First Roman Consul, he, too, said, "If I am guilty, needless to say, my head should fall; if my son is—I do not believe it, but, if he is,[52] *I, too, remember Brutus.*"

These horrible words, from which Nature revolts from the lips of a father, can be well believed from those of a *complaisant* husband;[53] but could the well-known virtue of Madame la Duchesse allow of such an explanation relative to her husband?[54]

To all these forcible arguments may be added one already mentioned, and which, after all that precede it, would be too extraordinary if it were the effect of pure chance.

I speak of the resemblance.

That of the present Duke to the various members of his supposed family is absolutely non-existent,[55] while he has all Chiappini's features: loose-hung jaw; tanned complexion; brown eyes; black hair; slightly crooked legs, etc.

As for myself, I can proudly boast that I have nothing in common with the former jailer; but every one is struck by the many points of resemblance seen between Mademoiselle d'Orléans and me—manners, tone of voice, physique, shape and colour of face, all identical.

I have the honour of bearing on my body certain marks distinguishing the late Dowager; at first sight her handwriting and mine display the most astounding similarity of character.

We need not add that whoever knows the history of Louis-Philippe-Joseph must have already discovered the disastrous source of the maladies I have suffered from since my birth, and that I have so unfortunately transmitted to my dear children, who themselves, in their turn, are the perfect image of the illustrious ancestors that I hold myself right in claiming.

What more could be wished for in the way of proof?

We must not lose sight of the fact that power and riches are two great means of corruption; that their own chief interests forced the perpetrators of the exchange to destroy as quickly as possible all essential traces of the deed; that fear and cupidity indubitably kept silent the greater number of witnesses, who, in any case, could not be very many, since, in 1773, they were already of a certain age, and fifty-seven years have gone by since then.

It must be remembered, also, that during this lengthy period took place that revolutionary tempest which spared private rights no more than public monuments.

Still, with lively gratitude, I say it once again, Providence has had compassion on me, and my latest investigations have furnished me with fresh pleas, which I feel I cannot with delicacy communicate to any one but my judges.

XIV

Objections and Answers — Chiappini's Ignorance — Name of the Maker of the Exchange — Prolonged Pregnancy — Absence from Paris — Motive of the Second Journey — Birth of the Duc de Montpensier and the Comte de Beaujolais — Letter dated from Turin — Apparent Contradictions — Virtues of the Duchess.

In setting forth the strong arguments in my own favour, I have also considered those that might be urged against me, and I hasten to answer them.

1st. "In his letter Chiappini said that I was born in a position almost similar to, but still lower than that given me by my marriage to Lord Newborough. Yet how great a difference between them! How superior was the first to the second, if I really had the honour of belonging to the august house of Orleans."

This mistake can be corrected in a few words.

Every one must see how extremely important it was to guard against any indiscretion on the part of the jailer, perhaps even such involuntary revelations as his pride in the lofty position of his son might draw from him.

Every sort of precaution, therefore, was taken to keep him in ignorance of the exalted rank of the Sieur de Joinville, whom he never knew but as a rich nobleman simply bearing the title of Count, a title so common in Italy that no one pays any attention to it, so to speak.

It was by this title he must have called my true father, in order to do away with milord's constant suspicions, when he came to London; and my husband, knowing more about the French nobility than he did, and having a notion that I might have its blood in my veins, gave me his commands, then so inconceivable, to avoid the great people of that nation,[56] fearing, no doubt, that some unlooked-for circumstance might let me discover my origin through them, which would infallibly have parted me for ever from him whose only means of overcoming my insurmountable repugnance was his perpetual references to the low estate from which he claimed to have raised me.

2nd. "Does it not seem strange that the Duc de Chartres, anxious to consign an atrocious crime to everlasting oblivion, should have assumed a name belonging to his family, and one so easily recognizable?"

There is nothing to prove that when he first came to live

at Modigliana, under the name of Comte de Joinville, he had formed the fatal plan. Perhaps the simultaneous pregnancy of his wife and Chiappini's may have really given him the first idea.

LOUIS-PHILIPPE, KING OF FRANCE

But let us suppose, as is more probable, that this hateful plan had been long made; how could he know what were the decrees of Providence?

The Duchess might just as well be about to give him a

boy as a girl. In that case, it would have been made public at once; Bishops, Cardinals, the Pope himself, would have been informed of it; a courier would have been dispatched to Versailles; the Prince and Princess would have excused themselves at Court by saying that the reason of their secret journey was to go to invoke the Virgin of Loretto for the granting of a happy *accouchement*, which they had believed would not take place for some months yet. Therefore a name not belonging to their family would not only have made them look foolish, but might have led to their being accused of falsehood, or have even given rise to legitimate suspicions.

3rd. "Why, even admitting the substitution, should the birth of the supposed Prince not have been immediately made public? Why bring back to France the reputed mother with the false appearances of a pregnancy which was made to last some months longer?"

An invincible sense of shame must necessarily have prevented a course which would infallibly have been taken in the absence of all fraud, under the hypothesis of deceit.

Not only was self-betrayal to be dreaded, but some possible imprudent talker; and after that there would be no way of concealing a secret that the mere inspection of the infants must reveal to the least skilful physiognomists.

The correctness of this conjecture was suddenly proved by experience; there is some indiscreet talk, and, in spite of the determined silence of the interested party, a little more and all would have been discovered. [57]

Hence a thousand anxieties, a thousand cares; [58] hence the absolute necessity of having recourse to expedients and thinking out new stratagems; and hence, above all, the very natural idea of putting a long interval between the real and the fictitious accouchement, so as to stop tongues, and, if need arose, to fall back upon the difference in dates.

4th. "Is it absolutely certain that the accused Prince and Princess were absent from Paris at the time of the exchange? The papers of the day seem to show the contrary. Do they not report that the Duke was in the Chapel Royal on April 8, being Holy Thursday; that, on the 13th of the following May, he accompanied his Majesty to the great review of the troops on the Plain of Sablons, and that in the month of June of that same year the Duchess was seen at the opera?"

We could, no doubt, content ourselves with sending our readers back to the unimpeachable testimony which has already vouched for the actual fact,[59] without taking the trouble to reconcile it with the vague and often incorrect assertions of many newspapers; but, for the sake of fuller proof, we are willing to discuss the matter briefly.

As to the Duchess, it is incontestable that her absences after the 10th of October, 1771, were so lengthy and so mysterious that certain historians, not knowing how to account for them, have maintained that she stayed at the waters of Forges during two consecutive years; while several eye-witnesses still living testify that she spent there only two of what they call their seasons, of about three weeks each.

It was on the 16th of June, exactly two months after my birth[60]—a time quite long enough for her return—that she was first seen at the opera. Monseigneur the Dauphin and Madame la Dauphine were expected; and the *Duchess de Chartres*, says a writer, *"had taken care to be in her box before the arrival of the august couple*; so much was she in doubt as to their demeanour towards her."[61]

It is equally well known that the Duke was not in Paris towards the end of May 1773, and that, failing him, recourse had to be had to the Princes of the house of Condé to appear

195

at the funeral-service for the King of Sardinia celebrated at Notre-Dame.

The list of assistants at the Holy Thursday ceremonies and at the Sablons review ought to be looked upon as mere official etiquette rather than historical and accurate reports of events; the constant uniformity during a long series of years to be noted is a convincing proof of this.

And even admitting that the Duc de Chartres was actually in Paris on Holy Thursday 1773, what does that prove?

At most that he was not at Modigliana the following Friday, the day of my birth.

But this, far from being against me, becomes, in a fashion, a presumption in my favour, as being absolutely in accordance with the deposition of the sisters Bandini, who swore to having seen the Sieur Joinville before and after the exchange, but said nothing of his being there on the day it was made.

What they said about that fatal day related to the Borghi family, the two children, the two mothers, even to Chiappini; the Comte alone is not mentioned.[62]

It might well be believed, then, that, the better to deceive inquiry, after having sealed his infamous compact, he went back to Court to perform his usual function at that sacred solemnity;[63] and, as he was an expert traveller, and even able to drive a chariot himself, it would have been still possible for him to start at once for the Apennines and get back there during the five weeks between the 8th of April and the 13th of May.

5th. "Supposing the Duke and Duchess of Chartres to have been the perpetrators of this abominable traffic, would the Duchess have returned to Italy three years later? Would she have reappeared under the same name of Comtesse

196

Joinville and with such a display of luxury and magnificence?"

Although at the time the Prince and Princess must have suffered from grave fears, they had, nevertheless, ground for hoping that influence and money would, if necessary, be able to stifle the accusing voices of a few poor and timid witnesses.

But could they be certain of equally good luck in the future?

Therefore it was necessary to think of and provide for everything. Well, what more efficacious and advantageous way of doing this was there than to put people on a wrong scent by confusing the dates? And supposing that some unlucky echoes of the old rumours at Brisighella and Ravenna[64] were still to be heard, what more likely to destroy them than boldness and bravado? What more plausible, deluding and beguiling than a visit in state after so short a lapse of time, a procedure which our opposers think so improbable?

In this matter we feel that the objection absolutely contradicts itself. Let us examine it in detail.

Nature does not easily give up its rights; it makes itself heard even in the hardest hearts, and the heart of a mother cannot possibly remain deaf to its mighty voice.

Therefore the Duchess's whole mind is drawn and attracted to the spot that holds the first-fruit of her maternity, and there is born in her the ardent desire to turn her steps thither.

Despite *convenances*, despite obstacles, despite a thousand objections, this desire must needs find fulfilment, with these two remarkable circumstances: *i.e.*[65] the first, that the Duke seems to have consented to his wife's request, only on the condition that she would bind herself in a very special fashion to keeping the secret inviolable by becoming a Freemason;[66] the second, that the arrival of the Princess at Florence exactly coincides with the time when great influence must have been used with regard to Chiappini, who was not only suddenly called to fill a more honourable and lucrative post, but was admitted to some sort of intimacy with his sovereign, who was good enough also to take a quite wonderful interest in me.[67]

Among the patrimonial estates belonging to the Orleans family, that of Joinville was the finest;[68] it was therefore the most natural name to take for an incognito; to choose another might possibly serve to increase the King's displeasure and to awake dangerous suspicions. Moreover, the correct pronunciation of the word is so strange to Italian lips that it was hardly probable that the wretched inhabitants of Modigliana would recognize it by the mere reading of the newspapers, which the greater number of them never saw.[69]

Finally, if Madame de Chartres displayed such magnificence and brilliancy in the places she condescended to visit, it was only to put every one on the wrong scent and the better to convince them that she had absolutely nothing to do with the simple and retiring lady so few people had seen some years earlier.

6th. "Supposing that Louis-Philippe-Joseph had determined on the substitution before his wife had given him a male child, would not the subsequent births of the Duc de Montpensier and the Comte de Beaujolais have induced him to make every effort to return the substituted child to its real position?"

But, admitting in our turn the possibility of such a reparation, there was always time enough to carry it out;

and it was expedient to make sure if the two first would live long; for, from their earliest years alarming symptoms must have given rise to very sad and, alas! but too true forebodings,[70] while the health of their *elder brother* was so assured and excellent that there was no need for fear about him.

A reputable personage wrote to us lately—

"I have been carefully examining the portraits of the present Duke of Orleans and of his two brothers, the Duc de Montpensier and the Comte de Beaujolais. There is a striking contrast between that of the first and those of the two others. In fact, the Duke of Orleans has, as is well known, a strong constitution, a robust temperament, and is common-looking, having coarse features.

"As for the two others, they look poor and weak in constitution and temperament, and of distinguished appearance, and bear no resemblance whatever to their brother," etc.

7th. "The Comte de Joinville wrote from Turin that, 'having lost the substituted child, he no longer felt any scruples on his account.'[71]

"Would there be any meaning in such words from the lips of the Duc de Chartres? Had he lost a single son in his life? Could this assertion relate to the Duc de Valois, who is still alive?"

Let us recall for an instant the insatiable avidity of the Chiappinis, and the whole difficulty will vanish. Is it not easy to believe that, far from satisfied with the considerable sums they had received from my father, and the annual pension handed over to them by the Countess Borghi, they must have kept up an incessant demand for more? Tired of the worry, Pompeo and his mother must themselves have begged the Comte de Joinville to write them a letter which would thenceforth put a check on the intolerable pestering of the *sbirro* and his wife. The style, the oddness, the curtness of this missive, all proclaim it the result of an arrangement between the two noble families. As it might always be of use, it was carefully preserved; the other portions of the correspondence might have been compromising, and were perhaps destroyed on the very day they were received.

8th. "According to the Signora Galuppi, the Duke and Duchess of Chartres had but few of their people with them at Reggio;[72] how, then, did the priest Brunone see them pass through Alessandria with a numerous suite?"[73]

To dispose of this contradiction—in itself proof positive that there was no plot or bribery—there are two ways of fully reconciling the double evidence.

1st. The Signor Brunone, living in a town far from Court-doings, may well have thought considerable what to a person living since her birth in a royal residence seemed insignificant.

2nd. Who knows if the Duke, when he started, did not leave in the Alps the greater number of the suite, which he took on again afterwards, so as to destroy any sign of his having anything whatever to do with a man who had been seen almost by himself on the other side of the mountains?

9th. "If it is easy enough to attack the memory of Louis-Philippe-Joseph, who does not know with what just and profound veneration that of his wife is looked upon, and which must, nevertheless, be tarnished by an accusation of unworthy complicity?"

No one can be more anxious than I to give the homage of my respect to the memory of the Duchess; and my dearest wish would undoubtedly be to believe a life made illustrious by its many virtues, without a stain. Indeed, I had at first tried to persuade myself that, having been once before the victim of deception, she had again fallen into the snare woven for her at the time of her first confinement.[74]

A consoling illusion, which the stories of witnesses and many other indications did but too quickly banish from my mind![75]

It is a well-known fact that the finest characters are not without defects, and no one who knew her could deny that the Princess was in truth very ambitious.

Moreover, the fact of her being her parents' only child and sole object of their deepest love, was an incentive for this loving daughter to turn her fondest hopes to the birth of an august scion who should be the glory of her maternity.[76]

Over this she ponders and frets incessantly, and, in the midst of her magnificent surroundings, she carefully *conceals the grief she feels at finding herself deprived of this blessing.*[77]

In consequence, she was naturally inclined to lend a favourable ear to the temptation offered her by a husband whom, besides, *she would not for all the world displease,*[78] and for whom her complaisance went so far as to help in the concealment of his vices,[79] even to the extent of uncomplainingly sacrificing not only *her tastes and her health,* but also *her warmest and most legitimate affections.*[80]

The crime once committed, she soon looked upon the wrong as irreparable, and from that time a false sense of honour, a deadened conscience, made it appear a duty to abstain from a revelation as degrading as it was unavailing.

CONCLUSION

Possibility, presumptions, relations of facts, statements by those who tell of what they have seen and heard; the absence of any interested motive for their assertions; such are the foundations, the elements of certainty, and it is by their means that two important facts have been proved: first, that of the exchange between the jailer Chiappini and the Comte de Joinville; secondly, that of the identity of the Comte with the late Duc d'Orléans-Egalité.

So I know who is my brother; I can name my mother; at last I belong to a family. Alas! shall I be for ever excluded, repulsed, from its bosom?

Shall I always be conspicuous as a witness to the truth that the Divine vengeance sometimes avenges the criminal's guilt even upon his unfortunate posterity?

I have been derided for my ridiculous credulity; accused of pursuing phantoms, of feeding on dreams and idle fancies.

Kind and attentive reader, you have seen, you have examined, the papers and the evidence I have submitted to you; you have considered and weighed them all; now give judgment, and condemn me if my documents are but lies, if my claims are but folly and wild extravagance.

But no! I dare to say your decision has been in my favour; and this flattering victory foretells for me the fullest, the happiest results.

No; it will not be in vain that I shall carry my humble supplications to the foot of the august throne where sits the most equitable as the best of kings; it will not be in vain that I shall lift my eyes and send forth my hopes to the sanctuary of justice; the throne will cover me with its beneficent shadow, and justice will give me the victory. Victory all the sweeter to my heart that then I shall be able to follow my love of liberality and benevolence without restraint or caution.

And what other compensation have I for so many perfidies and persecutions; for the long-drawn-out torture of the sad and solitary life to which I have been reduced?

Shall I be believed if I say that this profound sadness, this dark melancholy, that crushes and consumes me, does not arise solely from the vast abyss of my own misfortunes; it has, too, another cause in the cruel distress I have already inflicted on the involuntary usurper of so many rights which henceforth he cannot keep without guilt; for I know that she whom he wishes to appear so weak, and whom he affects to look upon with nothing but contempt, has troubled and frightened him; and, without knowing it, he proclaims and cries it aloud.[81]

And what especially increases my sorrow and completes my trouble is to think that that must fall upon a Princess so worthy of all respect and also upon the offspring of that venerable mother; and if I were thinking of nothing but my own interests, if I were the only person concerned, there would soon be a full and complete surrender.

But no! maternal love; the honour of my race; the glory of the most ancient of dynasties; all speak to me with their imperious voices, and how can I refuse the hard tasks imposed upon me?

Born of illustrious blood, my sentiments will always accord, always harmonize, with the loftiness of my origin.

It is true I see myself parted from my friends, separated from all I hold most dear on earth; I am alone, without stay or support; but the memory of my ancestors, the thought of my dear children, lead me on and rouse me to battle, and fighting under such banners how could I fail in courage or boldness? What greater proof of that boldness and courage could I give than my being here? I could have gone back to my adopted country, to the bosom of that tender mother, that gracious England to whom I owe an everlasting debt of love and gratitude.

From there I could have looked without terror upon the perils of the fight and seen the manœuvres of the enemy without fear of his darts. But I must always keep in the forefront of the battle, show myself in the breach, and guard against all blows.

Far from me be any shameful capitulation! May my hand perish rather than sign any degrading concession!

I have said it; I say it again, and shall constantly repeat it —

"To conquer, or die as I have lived. All or nothing!

"M. S. NEWBOROUGH, BARONNE DE STERNBERG,
NÉE DE JOINVILLE."

FOOTNOTES

[1] These documents, taken by M. Gaston Maugras from the papers of the Minister for Foreign Affairs (France, 319), have been published under the title of *L'Idylle d'une "Gouverneur," la Comtesse de Genlis et le Duc de Chartres.* (Paris, Librairie Plon, 1904.)

[2] This was extremely amusing to my lively companions, who could not understand such an occupation.

[3] This decision, given on December 17, 1822, was deposited, with the letter, with Maître A. Chelli, notary at Florence.

[4] These letters, which bore the Florence postmark, have always inspired me with very unpleasant suspicions as to the lawyer Chiappini.

[5] This, the 24th day of June, 1824, sitting in the name of our Lord, Pope Leo XII, the Sovereign Pontiff, happily reigning, in the first year of his Pontificate; declaration xii, at Faenza.

The period of ten days, in which to appeal, having elapsed since the notification of the judgment given by this Ecclesiastical Tribunal of Faenza, on the 24th of May last, in the lawsuit between her Excellency Lady Maria Newborough, Baronne de Sternberg, and M. le Comte Charles Bandini, of this town, acting as legal representative of the Comte Louis and Madame N. de Joinville, and to all such other absent person or persons who may have, or may suppose they have, any interest in the case; also to the Signore Dottore Tomaso Chiappini, living in Florence, in the State of Tuscany, without any one having appealed against it; I, the undersigned, by virtue of the faculties given me by the aforesaid judgment, have proceeded to the carrying out of that judgment, by means of the rectification of the birth certificate produced in the course of the trial, the terms of which are as follows:

"In the name of God, Amen.

"I the undersigned, Canon, Chaplain and Rector of the Prioral and Collegiate Church of St. Stephen, Pope and Martyr, in the territory of Modigliana, in the Tuscan States, and in the Diocese of Faenza, testify to having found in the fourth book of certificates of birth, the following notice:

"Maria-Stella-Petronilla, born yesterday, of the couple Lorenzo, son of Fernando Chiappini, Sheriff's Officer of this place, and Vincenzia

Viligenti, daughter of the late N. of this parish, was baptised on the 17th of April, 1773, by me, Canon Francesco Signari, one of the Chaplains.

"The god-parents were Francesco Bandelloni, Constable, and Stella Ciabatti.

"In testimony whereof, etc.,

"Signed, GAETANO VIOLANI,

"Canon, etc."

"Modigliani, April 16th, 1824."

"I have, I say, proceeded to the execution of the aforesaid judgment by carrying out the aforesaid rectification, which has been definitely made in the following form and words:

"Maria-Stella-Petronilla, born yesterday of the couple M. le Comte Louis, and Madame la Comtesse N. de Joinville (French) then living in the territory of Modigliana, was baptised on the 17th of April, 1773, by me, Canon Francesco Signari, one of the Chaplains. The godparents were Francesco Bandelloni, Constable, and Stella Ciabatti."

Signed, ANGELO MORIGI,

Registrar to the Episcopal Tribunal of Faenza.

[6] His wife.

[7] *The Princess Marie-Adelaïde de Bourbon-Penthièvre, who in 1769 married the Duc de Chartres, afterwards the Duke of Orleans, and surnamed Egalité, had, on the 10th of October, 1771, brought into the world a dead girl; and in 1773, though four years married, she had not yet the happiness of being a mother.*

It was on the 6th of October of this last year that it is said she gave birth to Louis Philippe, the present duke, successively called Duc de Valois, de Chartres and d'Orléans. On the 3rd of July, 1775, Madame de Chartres gave birth to a second Prince, to whom was given the name of Antoine-Philippe, Duc de Montpensier, who died in England on the 18th of May, 1807.

In the month of August, 1777, she experienced the joys of a double maternity by the birth of girl-twins, of whom one died of the measles when she was four years and a half old; the other, first called Mademoiselle de Chartres, is now known under the title of Mademoiselle d'Orléans.

Finally, on October 7th, 1779, she once more became a mother by the birth of another Prince, who was named Louis-Charles, Comte de Beaujolais, and died at Malta in 1808.

[8] The *Gazetta de Genova* of March 2, 1825.

[9] A man of the highest worth, to whom I owe the inestimable obligation of having, under circumstances I cannot mention, preserved for me the liberty and the life of my third son.

[10] The old Count George of that name, having defeated the law in his own country, took refuge in France with the abundant fruits of his vast depredations. Mr. William Stacpoole pursued him, and the mere sight of the French Courts of Justice brought about the famous transaction that made Cooper cry victory; he having taken the modest precaution to get previously from Mr. William the promise of a trifling gratuity of 800,000 francs as a reward for the trouble he was going to take in engaging an advocate to plead against Count George.

[11] Needless to say that they were in a pitiable state, and nearly useless.

[12] It is known that in 1782, the Duc de Chartres took them out of the hands of a man to entrust them to this *notorious* woman, and that this unprecedented innovation, which was in great part the cause of the subsequent differences between the Duke and his wife, was the occasion of many lampoons and satires. See the *Vie Politique de Louis-Philippe d'Orléans*, and other works.

[13] On the supposition that she had been the young Chiappini's foster-mother, it would be easy to understand why the eldest of her pupils constantly called her "mother," and why she herself spoke of him in so maternal a fashion. See the Journal of that *Prince* and several other works.

[14] See Cooper-Driver's "Answer to Madame la Baronne's Statement," etc.

[15] It would be truer to say "for the immense trouble he had given me."

[16] If by the title of Duc d'Orléans our correspondent means him who alone bore it at that time—that is to say Louis-Philippe, who did not die till 1785, we quite agree with him; but, in that case, we will ask him to take notice that that is by no means the person suspected of having made the exchange. If, on the other hand, he has heard speak of Louis-Philippe-Joseph, son of the former, then Duc de Chartres, and since so well known under the name of d'Orléans-Egalité, the sequel of our story must surely make him realize that the truth he has traced to its source is not quite so *true* a truth as he seems to believe. Let him read to the end.

[17] Those of the sham Duc de Normandie and the sham Baron de Saint-Clair.

[18] The first steward and the second lawyer of the Duke of Orleans.

[19] Alas! probability is not always proved true!

208

[20] *Conjuration de L.-P.-J.; Vie politique du même; Vie du Duc de Chartres*, and many other works.

[21] Every one knows of the sad fate of the unfortunate Prince de Lamballe.

[22] See *Explication de l'énigme*, and other works.

[23] See *Conjurations de L.-P.-J.; La Gazette de France*, and other works.

[24] "It is reported," says the *Gazette de Leyde* (article on Paris, July 23, 1773), "that M. le Duc de Chartres, under the name of the Comte de Joinville, is about to make a three weeks' visit to Holland."

The *Journal historique et politique des événements des différentes cours de l'Europe* (Article, *France*, Aug. 6, 1773), thus announces the carrying out of this plan: "Monsigneur the Duc de Chartres, having taken leave of the King and Royal Family, travelled to Metz, and from there to Thionville, from which place it is believed that Prince will go to Luxembourg and to the Austrian Netherlands, where he will travel under the name of the Comte de Joinville." We should like to know what the learned Laurentie could now plead in contradiction!

[25] See later, The Time and the Place.

[26] See the deposition of the Cavaliere Don Gaspar Perelli, son of the Governor of that town. Chapter III, Part II.

[27] *Conjuration de L.-P.-J.*, bk. I. It was this mask which, having sullied the natural whiteness of his skin, gave him his dark and brownish complexion.

[28] See *Conjuration de L.-P.-J.*, bk. I; *Vie Politique*, p. 6; *Vie du Duc de Chartres*, p. 25, etc.

[29] See the Journal of her life, and other works.

[30] Aglaé d'Este, daughter of the Duke of Modena.

[31] First with the Princess Mathilde d'Este, his sister-in-law, and then with *la belle Forcalquier*. See *Vie du Duc de Penthièvre*, by Maître Guénara, vol. i, pp. 45 and 114.

[32] See Chapter V, Part II.

[33] *Mémoires de Mme. de Genlis*, vol. iii, p. 14.

[34] *Mémoires de Mme. de Genlis*.

[35] *Ibid*. See also the *Gazette de France* and other works. As to the title of *Comtesse de Joinville*, the following letter, sent on May 15, 1776, by M. Roger de Jouscolombe, will be a sufficient explanation—

"MONSIEUR,

"I take the opportunity of the departure of M. Fontaine, private secretary to Madame la Duchesse de Chartres, to answer the letter your Excellency did me the honour to write to me the day before yesterday.

"I don't mention the day the Duchesse de Chartres, who starts to-morrow, will arrive at Reggio, because you will hear it from M. Fontaine; I confine myself to sending you below the list of ladies, gentlemen, and servants in the Princess's suite.

"I am delighted that this occasion has procured me the pleasure of receiving news of your Excellency; I should be still more so if you would entrust me with some commission that would let me prove by my alacrity in doing anything you would like the feelings of sincere and respectful attachment with which I have the honour to be, monsieur,

"Your Excellency's very humble and obedient servant,

"ROYER DE JOUSCOLOMBE.

"To His Excellency M. le Marquis Paoluni.

"List of the ladies, gentlemen, and servants with Madame la Duchesse de Chartres, travelling under the name of Madame la Comtesse de Joinville.

"To wit—

> Madame la Comtesse de Genlis.
> Madame la Comtesse de Rully.
> M. le Comte de Geils.
> M. le Chevalier de Foissy.
> M. Fontaine, Private Secretary.
> Four Chambermaids.
> Eight Footmen, or Servants.

"P.S.—Since writing my letter, Madame la Comtesse de Joinville, in consequence of the representations made to her as to the difficulty there would be in getting the necessary post-horses on the way, has determined to send M. le Chevalier de Foissy and M. Fontaine back to France with two servants. I thought I ought to warn your Excellency of this new arrangement, and I am going to hand over my letter to M. le Marquis de Clermont-d'Amboise, French Ambassador to Naples, who is starting for Reggio."

[36] The Duke of Modena was the maternal grandfather of Mme. la Duchesse de Chartres.

[37] *Mémoires secrets ou Journal d'un observateur,* etc., 29th July, 1771.

[38] *Journal historique,* vol. iv, and others.

[39] *Journal historique,* May 24. See Chapter XII, Part II.

[40] *Mémoires secrets ou Journal d'un observateur,* etc., June 21 and 28, and July 15, 1773.

[41] A town in Seine-Inférieure, where are the mineral waters the Princess went to drink after her marriage.

[42] He who is now called the *Duke of Orleans.*

[43] See the *Mémoires de la Genlis,* vol. iii; the *Journal* of Delille, and other works.

[44] *Mémoires de la Genlis,* vol. iii, p. 14.

[45] *Nouvelles historiques,* vol. ii, p. 311.

[46] First Part, Chapter X.

[47] See her correspondence with her husband, and the various lives of this last.

[48] The name by which he usually called his dear Comtesse de Genlis.

[49] *Journal* of the present Duke, March 25, 1791.

[50] *Ibid.*

[51] On almost every page of that memorial wherein he painted his own picture so well, with his religious and political opinions, there are such lively exclamations as, "Fine day! beautiful day! Splendid day spent at Belle-Chasse!" It was there la Genlis lived.

[52] This refers to the *eldest.*

[53] He was the husband of la Genlis!

[54] It is to be noted that when Orleans had finished speaking, a deputy called out to him, "You wretch! it will not be your first sacrifice of your family!" (*Conjuration de L.-P.-J.*).

[55] La Genlis herself says in set terms that, "*in looks he is very different from his brothers,*" and the comparison she makes is very far from being in favour of the first (*Mémoires,* vol. iii, pp. 150, 164, and following).

[56] See First Part, Chapter VI.

[57] See Chapter VII, Part II.

[58] Perhaps the many trips the Duke made during the summer of 1773, and on which he would take no more than two or three confidential followers (see *Gazette de Leyde,* August 6th, article, "Paris"), may have had for end nothing

but to ensure the success of his infernal project. And perhaps the child may have been deposited in one of those northern places the Prince so often visited.

[59] See Chapter XII, Part II.

[60] See Chapter I, Part I.

[61] *Mémoires secrets ou Journal d'un observateur*, June 16th, 1773.

[62] See Chapter II, Part II.

[63] See pages 123, 124, Part I.

[64] Chapter II, Part II.

[65] See Chapter XII, Part II, and *Mémoires de la Genlis*, vol. iii.

[66] *Journal de Delille*, Part I, Chapter VII, and *Mémoires secrets*, March 18th, 1876.

[67] See Chapter I, Part I.

[68] See the schedule drawn up at the period of the Revolution.

[69] Newspapers were very rare then, and the populace did not read them. Besides, the Italian papers said little about the Princess's journey; and it was only the *Gazette de France* that wrote about it at any length.

[70] See Chapter VI, Part II.

[71] See Chapter III, Part II.

[72] See Chapter XII, Part II.

[73] *Ibid.*

[74] We read in the *Muratore* that when it was seen that she had brought forth a dead child, a living one was hastily procured, and shown for a time to the Duchess, so as to spare her a sudden and dangerous grief.

[75] See Chapter II, Part II.

[76] See *Journal de Delille*, Part I, Chapter IV.

[77] *Ibid.*, Chapter V.

[78] *Ibid.*, Chapter VII.

[79] *Explication de l'énigme*, Part I, Book I.

[80] This is what she wrote to him on the subject of la Genlis herself: "Once more, *mon cher ami*, don't let us discuss my opinion of Mme. de Sillery. When I parted from her you did not attempt to justify her; you only said that *you had essential reasons for keeping to her*; and at least I rejoiced at the idea of *making a sacrifice for you that you would feel*" (See *Correspondance de L.-P.-J.*, p. 184).

Surely we may suppose that the important secret had something to do with these *essential reasons*.

[81] What, in fact, meant the many secret and ill-managed intrigues, the many spies; the many watchers of my doings; why the pains taken to seize books that were but now to be met with at every step? Why carry out these seizures not only in the provinces of this kingdom, but even in foreign countries—Germany, England, Switzerland, etc.?

RICHARD CLAY & SONS, LIMITED,
BRUNSWICK STREET, STAMFORD STREET, s.e.
AND BUNGAY, SUFFOLK.

A KEEPER OF ROYAL SECRETS

Being the Private and Political Life of Madame de Genlis

BY JEAN HARMAND

Price 15/- net

"Félicité Stéphanie de Genlis, comtesse, adventuress, governess, copious writer of novels, plays, and homilies, needed a biographer, and M. Jean Harmand has adequately supplied the want."—*Times*.

"Extremely interesting ... peculiarly vivid, and even fascinating ... he has made real for us the personality of Mme. de Genlis as that of a remarkable woman, who led a remarkable life."—*Daily Telegraph*.

"The true story of Mme. de Genlis's life—a story now fully set forth for the first time. And what an interesting figure she is now that we can see her clearly! 'A Keeper of Royal Secrets' runs to over four hundred pages, but few will find it too long."—*Daily News and Leader*.

"With the help of documents in the possession of the Genlis family, and of other materials obtained from a variety of sources, M. Harmand has been able to give us the first full-length portrait of the woman who witnessed the Ancien Régime, the Revolution, the Empire, and the Restoration, and who died under the July Monarchy."—*The Nation*.

"Deeply interesting ... she was an extraordinarily interesting woman, who lived in extraordinarily interesting times, and Jean Harmand has made the utmost of his long and deep study of both in this fascinating volume." — *Truth*.

"Highly interesting ... M. Harmand has produced much fresh material, and has made a most interesting addition to the inner history of nations." — *Liverpool Daily Post*.

At all Bookshops and Libraries

EVELEIGH NASH, 36 King Street, Covent Garden
LONDON, W.C.

AUTOBIOGRAPHIES

PUBLISHED BY MR. EVELEIGH NASH

THINGS I REMEMBER

By FREDERICK TOWNSEND MARTIN. 10/6 net.

MY PAST

By COUNTESS MARIE LARISCH. 10/6 net.

THINGS I CAN TELL

By LORD ROSSMORE. 10/6 net.

MY OWN STORY

By LOUISA OF TUSCANY, EX-QUEEN OF SAXONY. 10/6 net.

MY MEMOIRS

By MADAME STEINHEIL. 10/6 net.

MY RECOLLECTIONS

By the COUNTESS OF CARDIGAN AND LANCASTRE. 10/6 net.

MY MEMOIRS

By Princess Caroline Murat. 15/- net.

RANDOM RECOLLECTIONS

By R. Caton Woodville. 10/6 net.

THE AUTOBIOGRAPHY OF CHARLOTTE AMÉLIE, PRINCESS OF ALDENBURG

Translated and Edited by her descendant, Mrs. Aubrey Le Blond. 15/- net.

THE MEMOIRS OF MARIA STELLA (Lady Newborough)

By Herself. 10/6 net.

LEAVES FROM A LIFE

Anonymous. 10/- net.

FOXHUNTING RECOLLECTIONS

By Sir Reginald Graham. 10/- net.

IN THE DAYS OF THE DANDIES

By Alexander, Lord Lamington. 3/6 net.

MY MEMORIES

By the Countess of Munster. 12/6.

RECOLLECTIONS OF A MILITARY ATTACHÉ

By Colonel the Hon. Fred Wellesley. 12/6.

REMINISCENCES OF AN OLD SPORTSMAN

By W. B. Woodgate. 15/- net.

SPORTING RECOLLECTIONS OF AN OLD 'UN

By Frank N. Streatfeild, C.M.G. 7/6 net.

REMINISCENCES OF AN OLD 'UN

By Frank N. Streatfeild, C.M.G. 7/6 net.

HURRAH FOR THE LIFE OF A SAILOR

By Admiral Sir William Kennedy, G.C.B. Cheap Edition, 2/- net.

FORTY-FIVE YEARS OF MY LIFE

By Princess Louise of Prussia. 16/- net.

FORTY YEARS OF PARISIAN SOCIETY

By Arthur Meyer, Ed. of *Le Gaulois*. 10/6 net.

SOME REMINISCENCES

By Joseph Conrad. 5/- net.

MANY CELEBRITIES and a few others

By William H. Rideing. 10/6 net.

MY AUTOBIOGRAPHY

By Madame Judith (of the Comédie Française). 10/6 net.

Obtainable at all Booksellers and Libraries.

Eveleigh Nash, 36 King Street, Covent Garden, London, W.C.

————————

A FASCINATING BIOGRAPHY

THE MARRIED LIFE OF QUEEN VICTORIA

By CLARE JERROLD

Price 15/- net

"Full of interest ... it gives a lively glimpse, not only of Royal Courts, but of the manners of the time."—*Daily Chronicle.*

"It is a real gain to have a book like this, in which the truth is told, discernibly and even kindly."—SIR W. ROBERTSON NICOLL in *The British Weekly*.

"A bright, readable story of Victoria and Albert in their domestic and in their public life ... a clever and entertaining book."—*Liverpool Daily Post.*

BY THE SAME AUTHOR

THE EARLY COURT OF QUEEN VICTORIA

By CLARE JERROLD

Price 15/- net

"Of all the books dealing with Queen Victoria and her reign we consider this to be in all respects the best. Queen Victoria had a supremely difficult work before her, and did it extraordinarily well. And so has Clare Jerrold done hers."—*Graphic.*

"Excellent ... a book that strikes a distinctly human note."—*Birmingham Daily Post.*

"A lively and entertaining volume which will be welcomed by the generation that is growing up in ignorance of the details of the private life of the great queen."—*Guardian.*

At all Bookshops and Libraries

EVELEIGH NASH, 36 King Street, Covent Garden, LONDON, W.C.

www.ingramcontent.com/pod-product-compliance
Lightning Source LLC
Chambersburg PA
CBHW020610030726
47497CB00007B/2179